ADVENTURE STORIES FOR
FIVE YEAR OLDS

Helen Paiba is known as one of the most committed, knowledgeable and acclaimed children's booksellers in Britain. For more than twenty years she owned and ran the Children's Bookshop in Muswell Hill, London, which under her guidance gained a superb reputation for its range of children's books and for the advice available to its customers.

Helen was involved with the Booksellers Association for many years and served on both its Children's Bookselling Group and the Trade Practices Committee. In 1995 she was given honorary life membership of the Booksellers Association of Great Britain and Ireland in recognition of her outstanding services to the association and to the book trade. In the same year the Children's Book Circle (sponsored by Books for Children) honoured her with the Eleanor Farjeon Award, given for distinguished service to the world of children's books.

She retired in 1995 and now lives in London.

D0714632

Adventure

STORIES

for Five Year Olds

COMPILED BY HELEN PAIBA

ILLUSTRATED BY BEN CORT

MACMILLAN
CHILDREN'S BOOKS

For Raoul and Rachel with love HP

First published 2000 by Macmillan Children's Books
a division of Macmillan Publishers Limited
20 New Wharf Road, London N1 9RR
Basingstoke and Oxford
Associated companies throughout the world
www.panmacmillan.com

ISBN 978-0-330-39137-5

9 8

A CIP catalogue record for this book is available from
the British Library.

Typeset by SX Composing DTP, Rayleigh, Essex
Printed and bound in Great Britain by
Mackays of Chatham plc, Kent

Contents

The Martian and the Supermarket

Penelope Lively

It was the middle of the night when the rocket landed in the supermarket car park. The engine had failed. The hatch opened and the Martian peered out. A Martian, I should tell you, is about three feet high and has webbed feet, green skin and eyes on the ends of horns like a snail. This one, who was three hundred and twenty-seven years old, wore a red jersey.

He said, "Bother!" He had only passed his driving test the week before and was always losing his way. He was an extremely nervous person, and felt the cold badly. He shivered. A car hooted and he scuttled behind a rubbish bin. Everything looked very strange and frightening.

It began to rain. He wrapped himself in a newspaper, but the rain soon came through that. And then he saw that a sliding door into the back of the supermarket had been left a little bit open, just

2

enough for him to wriggle through.

It was warmer inside, but just as frightening. There were large glass cases that hummed to themselves, and slippery floors, and piles and piles of brightly coloured tins and boxes. He couldn't imagine what it was all for. He curled up between two of the humming cases and went to sleep.

He woke to find everything brightly lit. He could hear people talking and walking about. He tucked himself as far out of sight as possible. Feet passed him, and silver things on wheels. Once, one with a baby in it stopped just by him. The baby leaned out and saw him and began to cry.

"Ssh . . ." whispered the Martian. The baby continued to shriek until its mother moved the trolley on.

The Martian couldn't think what he should do. He was hungry and he wanted to go home and the

bright lights and loud noises in this place made him jump. He began to cry; tears trickled down his horns. He sniffed, loudly.

It was at this moment that a girl called Judy stopped right beside him. Her mother was hunting for fish fingers in the freezer and Judy was pushing the trolley and also wishing she could go home; she hated shopping. She heard a peculiar fizzing noise come from the gap between the fish fingers freezer and the one beside it, and looked in.

Plenty of people, looking between two freezers in a supermarket and seeing a thing there like a three-foot green snail with a red jersey on would have screamed. Or fainted. I think I would have. Not so Judy. She bent down for a closer look.

"Please don't tell anyone," said the Martian. "They might be unkind to me."

"Are you a boy or a girl?" asked Judy.

"I'm not sure. Does it matter?"

"Sometimes," said Judy, after a moment's thought. "It depends how you're feeling." She studied the Martian with care. "I think you're a boy. It's something about your eyes. Never mind. Some boys I quite like. How did you get here?"

6

"My rocket went wrong and I'd lost the map. Do you think you could help me get away?"

Judy thought about this. "I would if I could."

"I don't want to stay here," – the Martian's voice shook – "All these people make me nervous and the noise gives me a headache."

Judy looked round. Her mother had met a friend and was busy chatting. "Tell you what," she said. "Come home with us and I'll think of something."

"Will it be all right?" said the Martian doubtfully.

"I don't know," said Judy. "But let's try it anyway and see. Quick –

get into the box." Her mother had put a cardboard box into the trolley, ready to stack the shopping in. Judy looked round again – her mother was still chatting – grabbed the Martian, bundled him into the box and shut the flaps.

"I'm a bit squashed," said the Martian in a muffled voice. At that moment Judy's mother finished her chat and they were off to the meat counter.

When they got to the checkout Judy quickly grabbed another box and piled the shopping into that. Her mother, when she had found the right money and paid the girl at the till, was surprised they had enough to fill two boxes.

"It's always more than you think," said Judy cheerfully. She picked up the box with the Martian in it and carried it to the car.

At home, it was an easy matter to let him out while her mother was opening the door and whisk him round into the garage and behind the lawnmower. The cat, who had been sleeping there on an old sack, gave one look and fled, howling. It wasn't seen again for two days.

"Make yourself at home," said Judy.

"I'll bring you some lunch when I can. Sorry I can't ask you into the house, but you know what mothers are ..."

The Martian said he quite understood – he had one himself. "I don't want to be a nuisance," he added humbly.

She brought him beefburgers for lunch, which he liked, and sponge cake for tea, which he didn't, though he was too polite to say so. She also brought him some books in case he was bored, and before Judy's bedtime they played cards for a bit. The Martian was quite good at Snap, and even managed to win a couple of times. His horns went slightly pink when he was excited.

It is not the easiest thing in the world to keep a visitor of this kind in your garage without anyone else in the family knowing about it. Judy told the Martian to hide behind a pile of deckchairs when either her mother or her father came.

She and the Martian soon became fond of each other.

"If a person's nice," said Judy, "it really doesn't matter what they look like." Which was perhaps not the most tactful thing in the world to say, though she meant well.

"Thank you," said the Martian. "That's just what I've always felt myself." Truth to tell, he thought Judy was pretty odd-looking.

Judy was worried that he might be getting bored. It didn't seem any way to treat a visitor – hiding behind a lawnmower in the garage all day.

"Tell you what," she said, "my great-aunt's coming over this evening while Mum and Dad are out. You could come into the house and watch telly. She's so shortsighted she'd never notice you aren't one of my ordinary friends."

The Martian was doubtful. "Are

great-aunts fierce?"

"Not this one," said Judy.

So, that evening, Judy and the Martian sat on the sofa and watched telly while Great-Aunt Nora sat in the armchair and interrupted. She asked the Martian how old he was and what class he was in at school and where he went for his holidays last year.

"Jupiter," said the Martian shyly.

Judy gave him a nudge. "He means Cornwall, Auntie."

"That's nice," said Aunt Nora. She changed her reading-glasses for her other glasses and peered over at the Martian. "Have you been ill, dear? You're not a very good colour, are you? I think your mother ought to be giving you a tonic."

"He's had chickenpox," said Judy.

"Chickenpox was spots when I was young," said Aunt Nora, "not anything like he's got."

"There are horrible new kinds of chickenpox now," said Judy. Aunt Nora tutted and moved her chair a little further away.

The Martian quite enjoyed watching telly. He said he thought they used to have something like that where he came from back in the old days.

14

At nine o'clock, well before Judy's parents came back, the Martian slipped out to the garage again. Aunt Nora reported to Judy's mum that Judy's friend was a nice child, but a bit unhealthy-looking.

"Who was it?" asked Judy's mum. "Susie? Ben?"

"Someone new I've got to know," said Judy. Which was perfectly true. No more questions were asked, luckily.

On another day Judy managed to stay at home while her mother went to visit a friend. It was a sunny day and so it was a chance to get the Martian out in the garden for some fresh air. She bought them both an ice lolly from the corner shop and they settled down at the end of the lawn for a game of Snap. At which point, of course, the next-door neighbour, Mrs Potter, came out to hang up her washing and looked over the fence.

Judy hissed at the Martian to keep absolutely still. She went over to the fence and said good morning to Mrs Potter, specially politely.

Mrs Potter stared over the top of Judy's head. "My goodness, Judy, whatever is that? Sitting on the grass over there . . ."

"It's a garden gnome," said Judy promptly.

"Well!" said Mrs Potter. "I can't say I like the look of it much."

"Nor does Mum," said Judy. "She's sending it back. Don't say anything about it. She's a bit upset."

Mrs Potter nodded understandingly.

Judy, you will have realised, was someone who was pretty quick off the mark. Never at a loss. Even so, it was clear that things could not go on like this for ever. And the Martian was getting more and more homesick. Sometimes he sat behind the lawnmower quietly sniffing for hours on end. Judy felt really sorry for him.

She told the Martian that she would go to the supermarket with her mother the next day and see if his rocket was still in the car park.

The Martian brightened up. Then he said gloomily, "But even if it was, how would I get back to it?"

"I'll think of something," said Judy. "Don't worry."

But there was absolutely no sign of the rocket in the supermarket car park. Judy had a good look round while her mother was inside. Come to think of it, a small red rocket wasn't really the sort of thing that would have been left to lie around for several days. The question was – who had taken it and what had they done with it? She went into the supermarket to find her mother and help with the shopping.

When they got to the checkout her mother said, "Well! I see they've got something to amuse the toddlers now."

There, just by the exit, was the red rocket, mounted on a stand, sparkling with yellow lights and with a notice beside it saying TEN PENCE A RIDE. A mother put ten pence in the slot, popped her baby in the rocket and the rocket jiggled about and flashed its lights. The baby beamed out through the plastic hatch.

Judy stared. She hoped it wouldn't take off. But no – after a few minutes the rocket stopped jiggling, the mother lifted the baby out and put him in a pushchair.

As soon as she got home she rushed out to the garage to tell the Martian. He looked alarmed.

"This is terrible! If they haven't got it properly fixed it could take off."

"They think it's just a toy," said Judy.

The Martian got very distressed. "It's this year's model. Goes faster than sound if you want it to, not that I've ever dared. Something dreadful could happen if they keep it there."

Judy thought of babies whizzing out of the supermarket faster than sound. She nodded. Quite true – you could upset a person for life, having that sort of thing happen to them at that age.

"What we have got to do," she said, "is get *you* into it."

It would not be easy to get him back to the supermarket without Judy's mother noticing. Mothers, as you no doubt know, have a way of apparently paying no attention and then suddenly pouncing on anything unusual. But eventually they worked out a plan.

The next time Judy's mother was getting ready to go shopping Judy popped into the garage ahead of her, helped the Martian climb into the back seat of the car and bundled him up in her anorak.

When they got to the supermarket she tucked the whole bundle of anorak and Martian under her arm and carried it in after her mother. She was puffing and blowing with the weight. Her mother said, "Put your coat on – no need to carry it around like that."

"I'd be too hot," said Judy. One of the Martian's webbed feet was poking out. She tucked a sleeve round it.

"Suit yourself," said her mother.

The shopping seemed to take for ever that morning. First her mother forgot the eggs and had to go all the way back to the start to collect them. Then she met a friend. Then she couldn't decide what to have for supper. Judy staggered along behind. The Martian seemed heavier and heavier.

"Judy," said her mother. "Just run back and pick up another loaf, will you?"

Judy sighed. She walked back down the aisle. A woman with a

very full trolley, not looking where
she was going, came round a
corner smack into her.

"Oops!" said the woman. "Sorry,
love!"

Judy lurched into a mountain of
cornflake packets and dropped the
anorak. The Martian rolled out
and dived, quick as a flash, behind
a display of dustpans.

"Gracious!" exclaimed the
woman. "Was that your dog?
You're not allowed to bring dogs in
here, you know."

Judy could see the Martian
cowering behind the dustpans.

Several people had stopped to
see what the fuss was about. Judy

did some quick thinking. She took a deep breath and burst into tears.

"Ah . . ." said someone. "What's the matter, dear?"

"I've lost my mum," wailed Judy.

"Poor little soul," said another woman. "There . . . we'll soon find her."

Judy was the centre of attention. The Martian kept as still as still. Judy watched him out of the corner of one eye and went on crying with the other.

Her mother appeared round a corner. "Where have you been, for goodness' sake, Judy? And whatever's the matter?"

About five kind, motherly ladies

were patting Judy and promising to look after her. Judy wriggled free and flung herself at her mother. Everyone beamed, except Judy's mother, who knew Judy and didn't believe a word of it. She marked off towards the checkout with one hand firmly on Judy's shoulder.

As soon as they were standing in the line to pay, Judy cried, "Help . . . forgot my anorak . . . sorry . . ." and dashed back to the dustpan display. She scooped the Martian up in the anorak and came rushing back.

"Sorry about all this," she whispered. "Just hang on a bit

longer. Soon get everything sorted out."

There was a long line at the checkout. Judy could see the rocket flashing and jiggling. A baby was having a ride on it.

Judy slipped away from her mother and stood near them. Her mother was busy taking her shopping out of the trolley for the checkout lady. She looked up and said, "Judy! Don't go wandering off!"

"Just watching the rocket, Mum," said Judy.

The Martian poked one horn out from under the anorak and said, "I'm ever so nervous."

"So am I," said Judy. "The thing is, how're we going to get it off that stand they've put it on?"

The Martian peered a little further. "There are two screws. You'll have to undo them. Do you think you can?"

"I s'pect so," said Judy.

The rocket stopped jiggling. The mother lifted her baby out. Judy stepped forward and popped the Martian into the rocket, still wrapped up in the anorak.

"Giving your little brother a turn?" said the baby's mother.

"That's right," said Judy. "He's mad about space travel." She bent down.

"I shouldn't touch those screws, dear," said the woman.

"I'm just checking that it's safe," said Judy sternly.

Luckily the baby, who had caught sight of the Martian's horns, was now howling. Its mother turned away.

"I've done them," hissed Judy. "Are you ready?"

"All systems go," said the Martian. "That's what you're supposed to say, isn't it?"

"I think so," said Judy. She whipped her anorak off him and closed the hatch. "Well . . . Bye then. It's been ever so nice having you."

"Thank *you*," said the Martian. "I'll send you a postcard when I get back. Bye . . ."

Judy stepped aside and put ten pence in the slot. The rocket's lights flashed. It began to jiggle around and . . .

. . . Well, they are still talking

about it in the town where Judy
lives. At least those who saw it
happen are. Those who didn't, say
it was all imagination. But there
are at least twenty people who saw
a small red rocket go zooming
three times round the supermarket
and then out of the doors.

The local paper had a headline
that said MYSTERY BABY
TAKES OFF! And of course
nobody ever reported a missing
child. So after a while people lost
interest, though the supermarket
manager is still looking for that
toy rocket he found in the car
park. It had been very useful for
amusing the toddlers.

And after a couple of weeks Judy got a postcard of some very peculiar mountains, with stamps on the other side the like of which no one had ever seen.

Mrs Bartelmy's Pet

Margaret Mahy

High on a hill in her pointed house lived fierce little Mrs Bartelmy, who had once been a pirate queen. She lived there on her own with her gold earrings and wooden leg, and a box of treasure buried in her garden under the sunflowers.

Though she was fierce, Mrs Bartelmy often felt lonely. She was used to having lots of adventures.

She was used to the gay, wicked conversation of pirates. Now she lived on her own she often wished for someone to talk to.

"I could get a cat," thought Mrs Bartelmy, "but they are tame, sleepy animals. I am such a fierce old woman my cat would probably be scared of me. I wish I had been just a granny and not a pirate queen. Then a cat would love me."

Mrs Bartelmy was fond of sunflowers. She planted them all round her house. They grew so tall they almost hid the roof. One day when Mrs Bartelmy was digging among them she found the biggest cat she had ever seen sleeping there. It was a yellow cat with a small waist and tufted tail, and Mrs Bartelmy liked it at once. It had a golden mane round its face that reminded her of sunflowers. It yawned and showed its red mouth and white teeth. Then it smiled at Mrs Bartelmy.

Mrs Bartelmy went and brought it a big bowl of milk and a string of sausages. The cat lapped the milk. It ate all the sausages and growled fiercely.

"That's the boy!" said Mrs Bartelmy. "I like a chap who enjoys his food. You're fierce enough for me and I'm fierce enough for you. We'll get along together like a couple of jolly shipmates."

At that moment the gate squeaked. Mrs Bartelmy went to see who was coming. It was four men with huge nets and a fat man with a whip.

"We are circus men looking for our lion," said one of the men.

"The wicked, ungrateful animal has run away," said the fat man. "I am Signor Rosetta the Lion Tamer." He cracked his whip.

At the sound of the whip the big yellow cat leaped out, roaring ferociously. Mrs Bartelmy's big cat was a lion!

"You aren't to chase this lion,"

said Mrs Bartelmy. "He's a half-fierce, half-friendly lion and he's my shipmate."

"Well, you could have him," said Signor Rosetta, "but we need him for the circus, and we haven't got enough money to buy another lion."

"Is that all your worry?" said Mrs Bartelmy. She took her spade to a secret corner of her sunflower garden and dug up her chest of pirate treasure. She gave the lion tamer two handfuls of diamonds and Indian rubies.

"Is this enough to buy him?" she asked.

The lion tamer was delighted.

"It is enough to get three lions and two Bengal tigers. Ours will be the fiercest circus in the world!" he cried.

He went away and made the men with the nets go with him.

"That's that," said Mrs Bartelmy. Once the lion tamer, his whip and his nets were gone, the lion became gentle again and smiled at Mrs Bartelmy. It had flowers in its mane and smelled of new hay.

"Well, I never thought to get a cat so much to my liking," said Mrs Bartelmy. "I won't have to worry about scaring it when I get fierce, and it matches my sunflowers."

The lion and Mrs Bartelmy lived happily ever after. Often I have passed them, sitting on the doorstep of their pointed house among the sunflowers, singing with all their might:

Oh, there was an old woman
    who lived on her own
In a little house made from a
        smooth
    white bone.
And she sat at her door with a
    barrel of beer,
And a bright gold ring in her old
    brown ear.
And folk who passed by her

they always agreed,
That's a queer little,
  wry little,
  fierce little,
  spry little,
Utterly strange little
  woman indeed.

Teddy Robinson Goes to the Wrong House

Joan G. Robinson

One day Teddy Robinson got left behind by mistake at Auntie Sue's house. He had been there with Deborah and Mummy, and when it was time to go home he was dozing in the rocking chair, so nobody remembered about him.

When Auntie Sue came back from seeing the others off on the

train she found him sitting there all alone.

"Oh, poor fellow!" she said. "You've gone and got left behind. Whatever shall we do with you?"

Teddy Robinson couldn't think what ought to be done with him, so he didn't say anything.

"I think we'd better post you," said Auntie Sue. "I shan't be coming to your house for at least a week, and I'm sure Deborah will want you long before then."

So Teddy Robinson was wrapped in crinkly cardboard and a lot of brown paper, and Auntie Sue tied him up neatly with string. He made a very nice parcel indeed.

Then he was taken to the post office and handed over the counter.

Teddy Robinson thought this was the most exciting thing that had ever happened to him. He was longing to get home and tell everyone about his adventure, and he thought how jolly it would be to be able to tell a real travel story. He would start by saying, "When I was travelling by parcel post . . ." and then everyone would say, "Oh, yes, Teddy Robinson – do tell us about your adventure."

But it wasn't very exciting after all, because he was so well wrapped up that he couldn't see

what was happening to him.
Sometimes he seemed to be
bumping about in a sack with a lot
of other parcels, and sometimes he
seemed to be going smoothly along
in a car or a train. Then for quite a
while he seemed to be just lying
somewhere, not moving at all. And
it took a long, long time. Teddy
Robinson dozed, and woke up, and
dozed again.

At last he woke with a jerk. The
noise of a car engine had stopped,
and a chink of light was showing
through his brown paper.

"Hooray," said Teddy Robinson.
"I'm home at last. How surprised
Deborah will be to see me!"

But when he was unwrapped
Teddy Robinson found that he
wasn't home at all. An old lady
was looking at him, and she
seemed as surprised as he was.

"Well, now," she said, "whoever
can you be? And why have you
been sent to me?"

She felt all through the
wrappings of the parcel and all
over Teddy Robinson to see if
there was a letter to tell her who
he had come from. But there was
no letter anywhere. The old lady
smiled at him and stroked his fur
gently.

"You dear," she said. "I wonder
who you are."

46

Teddy Robinson saw that they were in a garden. The postman must have handed him to the old lady over the front gate, he thought. But why had he come to this house and not to his own house? He couldn't understand it at all. Nor could the old lady.

What had happened was that Auntie Sue had written the number of Deborah's house in a hurry. The number was thirty-nine, but because she was writing it quickly Auntie Sue made the three look like an eight; so Teddy Robinson had been sent to number eighty-nine in his own road instead of number thirty-nine. But

he didn't know this. Neither did
the old lady.

"I must ask the postman what to
do about you next time he comes,"
she said.

She began walking slowly up the
garden path with Teddy Robinson
in her arms. She stopped once or
twice to smell a rose, then she sat
him down on the front doorstep
and went round the side of the
house.

Teddy Robinson sat and looked
at the garden and thought about
how surprised he was to be there.

After a little while the old lady
came back wheeling a beautiful
big pram. She put it in the middle

of the lawn, then she looked up at the sky.

"It's a lovely afternoon," she said. "I think the sun's going to be quite hot."

She let down the hood and fixed a sun-canopy over the pram. It had a long silk fringe round it. Then she turned towards Teddy Robinson and smiled at him, shaking her head.

"I *wonder* who you can be!" she said.

She picked him up and carried him over to the pram. There was a soft woolly blanket inside. The old lady sat him on top of it, then she went indoors again.

"How very kind of her!" said Teddy Robinson to himself. "I've always wanted to sit in a pram under one of these sunshade things, and this is a fine one. It makes me feel like someone quite important."

He wished the hedge was low enough for him to see over into the road. He could hear footsteps of people passing by every now and then, and he thought how pleasant it would be to bow and smile at everyone from under the canopy as they passed by.

Soon the old lady came out again, carrying a rug, which she spread on the grass close to the pram. As she turned to go back she smiled again at Teddy Robinson and said, "Now, who can you belong to, you dear old thing? I *do* wonder who you are!"

The old lady said this so many times that after a while Teddy Robinson began wondering too.

I used to be quite sure I was me, he thought, but the old lady doesn't seem to be sure at all. And if I aren't me who am I? I wish Deborah was here to ask.

He began singing to himself, rather sadly, thinking round and round in his head about who he could be,

"If I aren't Teddy R,
then who can I be?
Who can I be
if I aren't really me?

"If I aren't Teddy R,
who everyone knows,
I'm some silly bear
who's got lost, I suppose.

"Some silly old bear
just sitting around,
who's nobody's bear
until he gets found."

"But if I aren't me," said Teddy
Robinson, "who is going to find me?
I don't want to be found by anyone
except Deborah. Oh, dear, I wish I'd
never gone in a parcel at all."

Just then the old lady came out again. This time she was carrying a little nursery-table, painted blue, with a chair to match. She set these down on the rug, nodded and smiled at Teddy Robinson, then went indoors again.

"She is going to a lot of trouble for me," said Teddy Robinson. "I've always wanted a little chair and table like that. I wonder what she's gone to fetch now."

Next the old lady brought out a playpen, and put it by the pram. Teddy Robinson was very pleased.

"I've always wanted a cage like that," he said, "so that I could play at being a fierce bear in the zoo.

53

She *is* a kind old lady."

After that more and more things were brought out and laid on the lawn. Teddy Robinson grew happier and happier.

There was a big animal picture book. ("Just the kind I like," said Teddy Robinson.) There were two deckchairs. ("One for her and one for me," said Teddy Robinson, "but I like the little blue chair best.") And, last of all, a tray of tea-things, and a big iced cake with three candles on it, and the name TEDDY written across the top in pink icing.

"Well, I never!" said Teddy Robinson. "Fancy her even

making a cake for me!" He began
singing a little song about all the
nice things the old lady was
bringing out into the garden.

"A chair and a table,
painted blue,
a very nice cage
and a picture book too,

55

a very nice cake,
a very nice pram –
what a very nice bear
she must think I am!"

Just then Teddy Robinson heard
more footsteps coming down the
road. Then suddenly his fur went
all tingly with excitement. He
heard Deborah's voice!

They must be coming to fetch
me, he thought, and was very
pleased to think he was found
at last.

But suddenly he began to feel
rather shy and silly.

"They'll wonder whatever I'm
doing here," he said, and decided

he would pretend not to notice them just yet. So he stayed sitting in the pram without moving, waiting until they were near enough to see him.

The footsteps stopped on the other side of the gate; then Deborah's voice, sounding very surprised, said, "Mummy! Isn't that Teddy Robinson?"

"It can't be, darling," said Mummy.

"But he's got Teddy Robinson's trousers on. Look!"

"*Has* he?" said Mummy. "Are you sure?"

They came nearer and peered over the gate. Teddy Robinson

stared hard at nothing, with his thinking face on.

"It *can't* be him," said Mummy. "How could he have got here? We left him at Auntie Sue's."

"But it's terribly like him," said Deborah. "I didn't think there could be another bear in the whole world that looked so like Teddy Robinson. I wish I could be sure."

"Oh, dear!" said Teddy Robinson to himself. "If even Deborah isn't sure I'm me perhaps I aren't me after all." And he began wondering all over again about who he could possibly be if he wasn't Teddy Robinson.

Deborah looked up at the

windows. Nobody was looking, so she opened the gate quietly and ran on tiptoe across the grass to the pram. She looked closely at Teddy Robinson with her head on one side, then she said, "You *are* Teddy Robinson, aren't you?"

"Oh, I hope I am!" said Teddy Robinson. "But I've had such a funny, bumpy, all-over-the-place sort of time just lately that I can't be sure of anything. If only you were sure I could be sure too. I do hope I'm me, and not just any old bear."

Deborah touched his ear gently with one finger.

"You *are* Teddy Robinson," she

said. "I knew you were! I can see Mummy's stitches where she sewed your ear on."

She ran back to Mummy, leaving Teddy Robinson where he was.

"It *is* him!" she cried. "Can I go and take him?"

"No," said Mummy, "we'd better not do that. You stay and talk to him while I go and ask."

So Mummy went up to the house and knocked at the door, and Deborah stayed on the other side of the gate and smiled at Teddy Robinson, and told him over and over again how pleased she was to see him.

"I feel rather sorry for the lady

who lives here," said Teddy Robinson. "She thinks I've come to stay and she's done such a lot for me. Look at this beautiful pram. She got it specially for me. And look at my beautiful cage over there, and my little chair and table – just what I've always wanted. And do you know – she's even made me a great big cake with three candles on it, and my name written on it in pink icing!"

Mummy and the old lady came down the garden path, laughing and talking together. Just as they were beginning to tell Deborah all about how Teddy Robinson had come by parcel post a taxi drew up at the gate.

"Oh, this will be my family!" cried the old lady. "You must stay and meet them. They've been away for a week. I've been so lonely without them."

A little boy got out of the taxi, followed by a lady with a baby in her arms.

"This is Teddy, my little great-grandson," said the old lady. "He is three years old today. You must all stay to tea, and help us eat the birthday cake."

So, after Mummy had said, "I don't feel we should . . ." and the old lady had said, "Oh, do," a great many times, they all sat down to

tea in the garden. The baby was
put in the pram, and the little boy
sat in the blue chair. Teddy
Robinson sat inside the playpen
and pretended to be a wild bear,
but he was too happy to look very
fierce.

They had a lovely tea party.
When it was time to go home the
old lady said, "I hope you will all
come again – Teddy Robinson too."
And Deborah said, "Thank you
very much. We will."

As they walked up the road to
their own house again Deborah
said, "Dear Teddy Robinson, I'm
so glad you've come back. It's been
horrid without you."

"Yes, hasn't it?" said Teddy Robinson. "And wasn't it lucky those children came to stay with the old lady just when they did? She won't miss me nearly so much now. The baby can use my pram, and the little boy can have my chair. It was very kind of her to give me all those nice things, but I'd *much* rather be found again and know I really am Teddy Robinson."

And that is the end of the story about how Teddy Robinson went to the wrong house.

Daft Jack and the Bean Stack

Laurence Anholt

Daft Jack and his mother were so poor . . . they lived under a cow in a field. His mum slept at the front end . . . and Jack slept at the udder end.

Daisy was a good cow, but the problem was, Jack's mum was fed up with milk. It was all they ever had —

hot milk,

cold milk,

warm milk,

milk on toast,

milk pudding.

And on Sundays, for a special treat, they had Milk Surprise (which was really just milk with milk on top).

Jack didn't mind milk, but his mother would have given anything for a change.

"I'M SICK AND TIRED OF MILK!" she would shout. "If I never taste another drop as long as I live it will be too soon. If only you were a clever boy, Jack, you would think of something."

"I have thought of something," said Jack. "It's a new kind of milkshake – it's milk flavoured."

Jack's mum chased him all around the field.

One day, a terrible thing happened; Jack was sitting in the field eating a Mini Milk lolly and his mum was having her afternoon rest when Daisy suddenly looked up at the grey sky, decided it was going to rain and, as all cows do, lay down.

"Right! That is it. I've had enough!" spluttered Jack's mum when Jack had pulled her out by the ankles. "You will have to take Daisy into town and sell her. But

67

make sure you get a good price or
I'll chase you around the field for a
week."

Daft Jack was very sad because
Daisy was more like a friend than
just a roof over his head. But he
always liked to please his mother.

He made himself a milk
sandwich for the journey and Jack

and Daisy set off towards the town. It was a long way so they took it in turns to carry each other.

Then at the top of a hill, they met an old man sitting on a tree stump with a shopping bag.

"That's a fine cow you're carrying," he said. "What's your name, sonny?"

"It's Jack," said Jack, "but everyone calls me 'Daft', I don't know why."

"Well, Jack," said the old man. "I'd like to buy that cow from you."

"I would like to sell this cow too," said Jack, "but you'll have to give me a good price for her.

Otherwise my mum will chase me around the field for a week."

"I can see you're a clever boy," said the old man, "and I'm in a good mood today. So guess what I'm going to give you for that cow?"

"What?" said Jack.

The old man reached into his shopping bag.

"Beans!" said the old man. "Not just one bean! Not just two beans! I'm going to give you A WHOLE TIN OF BAKED BEANS."

Jack couldn't believe his luck. Not one bean, not two beans, but a WHOLE TIN of baked beans for just one old cow. It must have been his lucky day. At last his mum would be proud of him.

So Jack kissed Daisy goodbye and set off home carrying the tin of beans as carefully as he would carry a newborn baby, feeling very pleased with himself.

As soon as he saw the field he began to shout, "Look, Mum! All our troubles are over. Guess what I got for Daisy? Not one bean. Not two beans. But A WHOLE TIN COMPLETELY FULL OF BEANS! Why, Mother, there must be A HUNDRED yummy beans in this tin. I knew you'd be pleased."

At the end of the week, when his mum had finished chasing him,

Daft Jack and his mum sat down in the middle of the field.

"Oh Jack," wailed his mum. "Now we haven't even got a cow to sleep under. If only you were a clever boy, you'd think of something."

"I have thought of something, Mum," said Jack. "Let's eat the beans."

So Daft Jack and his mum ate the beans. Then they had nothing left at all.

That night, Jack couldn't sleep. "I can't do anything right," he thought sadly. "My poor mother would be better off without me. I think I will run away into the big wide world and seek my fortune."

So Jack decided to leave a note for his mother. He couldn't find any paper so he tore the label from the bean tin. But there was something already written on the back of the baked bean label.

Jack held the paper up to the moonlight and read aloud:

"CONGRATULATIONS!
You have bought
THE LUCKY BEAN TIN
and won a
FANTASTIC PRIZE
for you and
your family!"

Jack woke up his mother. When

she saw the message on the bean
tin, she couldn't believe her eyes.
"Oh Jack," she cried. "At last we
will be able to buy a proper house."

"Yes," said Jack, "and I will buy
poor Daisy back. I fancy a nice
glass of milk."

And Jack's mum was too happy
to chase him around the field.

In the morning they sent off the
lucky bean label and soon their
prize arrived – A WHOLE
LORRY-LOAD OF BAKED
BEANS.

Jack and his mum didn't know
what to say. They began to stack
the tins in one corner of the field,
but before they had finished a

second lorry-load of beans arrived.

And all day long the lorries kept coming.

By the evening there was a huge pile of bean tins. A STACK of bean tins. A COLOSSAL GLEAMING MONUMENTAL MOUNTAIN of bean tins. There were bean tins right up to the clouds.

So from that day Daft Jack and his mum ate beans. It was all they ever had –
hot beans,
cold beans,
warm beans,
beans on toast,
bean pudding.

And on Sundays, for a special treat, they had Bean Surprise (which was really just beans with beans on top).

Jack's mum would have given anything for a change.

"I'm SICK AND TIRED OF BEANS!" she shouted one day. "If I never eat another bean as long as I live it will be too soon. If only you were a clever boy, Jack, you would think of something."

"I have thought of something," said Jack. "Bean juice milkshake."

There wasn't room to chase Jack around the field because the bean stack was too big. So Jack's mum chased him up the bean stack instead.

Higher and higher, Jack hopped from tin to tin with his mum puffing and panting behind.

Until at last Jack climbed so high, he left his mum far behind. But Jack didn't stop. He kept on climbing. He looked down at the world below. He saw the field as small as a handkerchief and his mum as tiny as an ant. And still Jack climbed higher.

When he was almost too tired to climb any more, Jack reached the top of the bean stack, way up in the clouds.

Jack looked around. To his

amazement he saw an enormous castle with its great door wide open.

He tiptoed inside. It was the most incredible place he had ever seen.

Jack wandered from room to room. He found massive bedrooms with carpets as thick as snowdrifts, a solar-heated Jacuzzi, a living room with great armchairs and a TV screen the size of a cinema.

At last, Jack wandered into a wonderful kitchen fitted with every kind of gadget.

Jack was interested in cooking and he climbed up to look at the giant-sized microwave.

Suddenly, the whole castle began to shake. A great voice roared.

"FEE, FI, FO, FUM, I've got a giant pain in my tum!"

Jack looked around in alarm and saw an enormous giant sitting at a table, rubbing his stomach and looking very miserable.

"S' not fair!" complained the giant. "All I ever get to eat is CHILDREN! And now I've got belly ache . . .
hot kids,
cold kids,
warm kids,
kids on toast,
kid pudding.

And on Sundays, for a special treat, I have Kid Surprise (but that's just kids with kids on top). I'd give ANYTHING for a change. I'M SICK AND TIRED OF KIDS! If I never ate another kid as long as I live it would be too soon . . ." He looked down at Jack. "AND NOW I'VE GOT TO EAT

YOU TOO! S'NOT FAIR!"

The giant reached out a huge hairy hand and grabbed Jack around the waist.

He lifted Jack kicking and struggling into the air and opened his vast black cave-like mouth with a tongue like a huge purple carpet.

"Well," thought Jack, "this is the end of Daft Jack and no mistake."

He was just about to be crunched into a million tiny daft pieces, when suddenly he had an idea.

"Er, excuse me, Mr Giant," he whispered nervously. "If you eat me it will only make your tummy ache worse. I can think of something much nicer. I don't suppose you like . . . beans, do you?"

"BEANS!" roared the giant. "DO I LIKE BEANS? I YUMMY YUMMY LOVE 'em!"

So Jack took the giant by the hand and led him down the bean stack. And on the way, the giant told Jack how lonely he was, all by himself in the great big castle in the clouds with nothing to do but eat people.

Jack began to feel very sorry for the poor giant and took him home to meet his mum.

"Oh, Jack," she cried. "Wherever have you bean?"

Jack's mum was very pleased to see Jack in one piece. But when she saw the giant . . . !

And when the giant saw Jack's mum . . . !

It was love at first sight.

"FEE, FI, FO, FUM, I'm going to marry Daft Jack's mum!"

"Of course you are, dear," said Jack's mum, "but first you must be hungry after your long journey."

The giant looked at the bean stack, gleaming in the evening light and he licked his giant lips.

"FUM, FO, FEE, FI, I wanna a giant-sized baked bean pie!"

He began munching the beans. Not one tin, not two tins, but the whole stack of beans. And he didn't even stop to open the tins.

So Daft Jack's mum married the giant, and they were very happy. They all went to live in the giant's wonderful castle in the sky.

Daft Jack opened a café in the giant's kitchen and he called it "DAFT JACK'S SKY SNACKS". And people came from far and wide and Jack grew rich and happy.

He served everything you can think of except milk . . .

and beans!

Clever Polly and the Stupid Wolf

Catherine Storr

Once every two weeks Polly went over to the other side of the town to see her grandmother. Sometimes she took a small present, and sometimes she came back with a small present for herself. Sometimes all the rest of the family went too, and sometimes Polly went alone.

One day, when she was going by herself, she had hardly got down the front door steps when she saw the wolf.

"Good afternoon, Polly," said the wolf. "Where are you going to, may I ask?"

"Certainly," said Polly. "I'm going to see my grandma."

"I thought so!" said the wolf, looking very much pleased. "I've been reading about a little girl who went to visit her grandmother and it's a very good story."

"Little Red Riding Hood?" suggested Polly.

"That's it!" cried the wolf. "I read it out loud to myself as a bedtime story. I did enjoy it. The wolf eats up the grandmother, *and* Little Red Riding Hood. It's almost the only story where a wolf really gets anything to eat," he added sadly.

"But in my book he doesn't get Red Riding Hood," said Polly. "Her father comes in just in time to save her."

"Oh, he doesn't in *my* book!" said the wolf. "I expect mine is the true story, and yours is just invented. Anyway, it seems a good idea."

"What is a good idea?" asked Polly.

"To catch little girls on their way to their grandmothers' cottages,"

87

said the wolf. "Now where had I got to?"

"I don't know what you mean," said Polly.

"Well, I'd said, 'Where are you going to?'" said the wolf. "Oh yes. Now I must say, 'Where does she live?' Where does your grandmother live, Polly Riding Hood?"

"Over the other side of the town," answered Polly.

The wolf frowned.

"It ought to be 'Through the Wood'," he said. "But perhaps town will do. How do you get there, Polly Riding Hood?"

"First I take a train and then I

take a bus," said Polly.

The wolf stamped his foot.

"No, no, no, no!" he shouted.
"That's all wrong. You can't say
that. You've got to say, 'By that
path winding through the trees',
or something like that. You can't
go by trains and buses and things.
It isn't fair."

"Well, I could say that," said
Polly, "but it wouldn't be true. I do
have to go by bus and train to see
my grandma, so what's the good of
saying I don't?"

"But then it won't work," said
the wolf impatiently. "How can I
get there first and gobble her up
and get all dressed up to trick you

89

into believing I am her, if we've
got a great train journey to do?
And anyhow I haven't any money
on me, so I can't even take a ticket.
You just can't say that."

"All right, I won't say it," said
Polly agreeably. "But it's true all
the same. Now just excuse me,

Wolf, I've got to get down to the station because I am going to visit my grandma even if you aren't."

The wolf slunk along behind Polly, growling to himself. He stood just behind her at the booking-office and heard her ask for her ticket, but he could not go any further. Polly got into a train and was carried away, and the wolf went sadly home.

But just two weeks later the wolf was waiting outside Polly's house again. This time he had plenty of change in his pocket. He even had a book tucked under his front leg to read in the train.

He partly hid himself behind a

corner of brick wall and watched
to see Polly come out on her way
to her grandmother's house.

But Polly did not come out
alone, as she had before. This time
the whole family appeared, Polly's
father and mother too. They got
into the car which was waiting in
the road, and Polly's father started
the engine.

The wolf ran along behind his
brick wall as fast as he could, and
was just in time to get out into the
road ahead of the car, and to stand
waving his paws as if he wanted a
lift as the car came up.

Polly's father slowed down, and
Polly's mother put her head out

of the window.

"Where do you want to go?" she asked.

"I want to go to Polly's grandmother's house," the wolf answered. His eyes glistened as he looked at the family of plump little girls in the back of the car.

"That's where we are going," said her mother, surprised. "Do you know her then?"

"Oh no," said the wolf. "But you see, I want to get there very quickly and eat her up and then I can put on her clothes and wait for Polly, and eat her up too."

"Good heavens!" said Polly's father. "What a horrible idea! We certainly shan't give you a lift if that is what you are planning to do."

Polly's mother wound up the window again and Polly's father drove quickly on. The wolf was left standing miserably in the road.

"Bother!" he said to himself angrily. "It's gone wrong again. I can't think why it can't be the same as the Little Red Riding Hood story. It's all these buses and cars and trains that make it go wrong."

But the wolf was determined to get Polly, and when she was due to visit her grandmother again, a fortnight later, he went down and took a ticket for the station he had heard Polly ask for. When he got out of the train, he climbed on a bus, and soon he was walking down the road where Polly's grandmother lived.

"Aha!" he said to himself, "this time I shall get them both. First the grandma, then Polly."

He unlatched the gate into the garden, and strolled up the path to Polly's grandmother's front door. He rapped sharply with the knocker.

"Who's there?" called a voice from inside the house.

The wolf was very much pleased. This was going just as it had in the story. This time there would be no mistakes.

"Little Polly Riding Hood," he said in a squeaky voice. "Come to see her dear grandmother, with a little present of butter and eggs and – er – cake!"

There was a long pause. Then the voice said doubtfully. "*Who* did you say it was?"

"Little Polly Riding Hood," said the wolf in a great hurry, quite forgetting to disguise his voice this time. "Come to eat up her dear grandmother with butter and eggs!"

There was an even longer pause. Then Polly's grandmother put her head out of a window and looked down at the wolf.

"I beg your pardon?" she said.

"I am Polly," said the wolf firmly.

"Oh," said Polly's grandmother. She appeared to be thinking hard. "Good afternoon, Polly. Do you know if anyone else happens to be coming to see me today? A wolf, for instance?"

"No. Yes," said the wolf in great confusion. "I met a Polly as I was coming here – I mean, I, Polly, met a wolf on my way here, but she can't have got here yet because I started specially early."

"That's very queer," said the grandma. "Are you quite sure

you are Polly?"

"Quite sure," said the wolf.

"Well, then, I don't know who it is who is here already," said Polly's grandmother. "She said she was Polly. But if you are Polly then I think this other person must be a wolf."

"No, no, I am Polly," said the

wolf. "And, anyhow, you ought not to say all that. You ought to say, 'Lift the latch and come in.'"

"I don't think I'll do that," said Polly's grandma. "Because I don't want my nice little Polly eaten up by a wolf, and if you come in now the wolf who is here already might eat you up."

Another head looked out of another window. It was Polly's.

"Bad luck, Wolf," she said. "You didn't know that I was coming to lunch and tea today instead of just tea as I generally do – so I got here first. And as you are Polly, as you've just said, I must be the wolf, and you'd better run away quickly before I gobble you up, hadn't you?"

"Bother, bother, bother and *bother*!" said the wolf. "It hasn't worked out right this time either. And I did just what it said in the book. Why can't I ever get you, Polly, when that other wolf managed to get his little girl?"

"Because this isn't a fairy story," said Polly, "and I'm not Little Red Riding Hood, I am Polly and I can always escape from you, Wolf, however much you try to catch me."

"Clever Polly," said Polly's grandma. And the wolf went growling away.

Down the Hill

Arnold Lobel

Frog knocked at Toad's door.
"Toad, wake up," he cried.
"Come out and see how wonderful
the winter is!"

"I will not," said Toad. "I am in
my warm bed."

"Winter is beautiful," said Frog.
"Come out and have fun."

"Blah," said Toad. "I do not have
any winter clothes."

Frog came into the house. "I

have brought you some things to wear," he said. Frog pushed a coat down over the top of Toad. Frog pulled snowpants up over the bottom of Toad. He put a hat and scarf on Toad's head.

"Help!" cried Toad. "My best friend is trying to kill me!"

"I am only getting you ready for winter," said Frog.

Frog and Toad went outside. They tramped through the snow.

"We will ride down this big hill on my sledge," said Frog.

"Not me," said Toad.

"Do not be afraid," said Frog. "I will be with you on the sledge. It will be a fine, fast ride. Toad, you

sit in front. I will sit just behind
you."

The sledge began to move down
the hill.

"Here we go!" said Frog.

There was a bump. Frog fell off
the sledge. Toad rushed past trees
and rocks.

"Frog, I am glad that you are
here," said Toad. Toad leaped over
a snowdrift. "I could not steer the
sledge without you, Frog," he said.
"You are right. Winter is fun!"

A crow flew nearby.

"Hello Crow," shouted Toad.
"Look at Frog and me. We can ride
a sledge better than anybody in
the world!"

"But Toad," said the crow, "you are alone on the sledge."

Toad looked round. He saw that Frog was not there. "I AM ALONE!" screamed Toad.

Bang!

The sledge hit a tree.

Thud!

The sledge hit a rock.

Plop!

The sledge dived into the snow.

Frog came running down the hill. He pulled Toad out of the snow. "I saw everything," said Frog. "You did very well by yourself."

"I did not," said Toad. "But there is one thing that I can do all by myself."

"What is that?" asked Frog.

"I can go home," said Toad.

"Winter may be beautiful but bed is much better."

The Baker's Cat

Joan Aiken

Once there was an old lady, Mrs Jones, who lived with her cat, Mog. Mrs Jones kept a baker's shop, in a little tiny town, at the bottom of a valley between two mountains.

Every morning you could see Mrs Jones's light twinkle on, long before all the other houses in the town, because she got up very early to bake loaves and buns and jam tarts and Welsh cakes.

First thing in the morning Mrs Jones lit a big fire. Then she made dough, out of flour and water and sugar and yeast. Then she put the dough into pans and set it in front of the fire to rise.

Mog got up early too. He got up to catch mice. When he had chased all the mice out of the bakery, he wanted to sit in front of the warm fire. But Mrs Jones wouldn't let him, because of the loaves and buns there, rising in their pans.

She said, "Don't sit on the buns, Mog."

The buns were rising nicely. They were getting fine and big.

That is what yeast does. It makes bread and buns and cakes swell up and get bigger and bigger.

As Mog was not allowed to sit by the fire, he went to play in the sink.

Most cats hate water, but Mog didn't. He loved it. He liked to sit by the tap, hitting the drops with his paw as they fell, and getting water all over his whiskers!

What did Mog look like? His back, and his sides, and his legs down as far as where his socks would have come to, and his face and ears and his tail were all marmalade-coloured. His stomach and his waistcoat and his paws

were white. And he had a white
tassel at the tip of his tail, white
fringes to his ears, and white
whiskers. The water made his
marmalade fur go almost fox-
colour and his paws and waistcoat
shining-white clean.

But Mrs Jones said, "Mog, you
are getting too excited. You are
shaking water all over my pans of
buns, just when they are getting
nice and big. Run along and play
outside."

Mog was affronted. He put his
ears and tail down (when cats are
pleased they put their ears and
tails up) and went out. It was
raining hard.

A rushing rocky river ran through the middle of the town. Mog went and sat in the water and looked for fish. But there were no fish in that part of the river. Mog got wetter and wetter. But he didn't care. Presently he began to sneeze.

Then Mrs Jones opened her door and called, "Mog! I have put the buns in the oven. You can come in now, and sit by the fire."

Mog was so wet that he was shiny all over, as if he had been polished. As he sat by the fire he sneezed nine times.

Mrs Jones said, "Oh dear, Mog, are you catching a cold?"

She dried him with a towel and gave him some warm milk with yeast in it. Yeast is good for people when they are poorly.

Then she left him sitting in front of the fire and began making jam tarts. When she had put the tarts in the oven she went out shopping, taking her umbrella.

But what do you think was happening to Mog?

The yeast was making him rise.

As he sat dozing in front of the lovely warm fire he was growing bigger and bigger.

First he grew as big as a sheep.

Then he grew as big as a donkey.

Then he grew as big as a carthorse.

Then he grew as big as a hippopotamus.

By now he was too big for Mrs Jones's little kitchen, but he was far too big to get through the door. He just burst the walls.

When Mrs Jones came home

with her shopping bag and her umbrella she cried out, "Mercy me, what is happening to my house?"

The whole house was bulging. It was swaying. Huge whiskers were poking out of the kitchen window. A marmalade-coloured paw came out of one bedroom window, and an ear with a white fringe out of the other.

"Morow?" said Mog. He was waking up from his nap and trying to stretch.

Then the whole house fell down.

"Oh, Mog!" cried Mrs Jones. "Look what you've done."

The people in the town were very

astonished when they saw what
had happened.

They gave Mrs Jones the Town
Hall to live in, because they were
so fond of her (and her buns). But
they were not so sure about Mog.

The Mayor said, "Suppose he
goes on growing and breaks our
Town Hall? Suppose he turns
fierce? It would not be safe to have
him in the town, he is too big."

Mrs Jones said, "Mog is a gentle
cat. He would not hurt anybody."

"We will wait and see about
that," said the Mayor. "Suppose he
sat down on someone? Suppose he
was hungry? What will he eat? He
had better live outside the town,

up on the mountain."

So everybody shouted, "Shoo! Scram! Psst! Shoo!" and poor Mog was driven outside the town gates. It was still raining hard. Water was rushing down the mountains. Not that Mog cared.

But poor Mrs Jones was very sad. She began making a new lot of loaves and buns in the Town Hall, crying into them so much that the dough was too wet, and very salty.

Mog walked up the valley between the two mountains. By now he was bigger than an elephant – almost a big as a whale! When the sheep on the mountain saw him coming, they were scared to death and galloped away. But he took no notice of them. He was looking for fish in the river. He caught lots of fish! He was having a fine time.

By now it had been raining for so long that Mog heard a loud, watery roar at the top of the valley. He saw a huge wall of water coming towards him. The river was beginning to flood, as more and more rainwater poured down into it, off the mountains.

Mog thought, "If I don't stop that water, all these fine fish will be washed away."

So he sat down, plump in the

middle of the valley, and he spread himself out like a big, fat cottage loaf.

The water could not get by.

The people in the town had heard the roar of the floodwater. They were very frightened. The Mayor shouted, "Run up the mountains before the water gets to the town, or we shall all be drowned!"

So they all rushed up the mountains, some on one side of the town, some on the other.

What did they see then?

Why, Mog sitting in the middle of the valley. Beyond him was a great lake.

"Mrs Jones," said the Mayor, "can you make your cat stay there till we have built a dam across the valley, to keep all that water back?"

"I will try," said Mrs Jones. "He mostly sits still if he is tickled under his chin."

So for three days everybody in the town took turns tickling Mog under his chin with hay-rakes. He purred and purred and purred. His purring made big waves roll right across the lake of floodwater.

All this time the best builders were making a great dam across the valley.

People brought Mog all sorts of

nice things to eat, too – bowls of cream and condensed milk, liver and bacon, sardines, even chocolate! But he was not very hungry. He had eaten so much fish.

On the third day they finished the dam. The town was safe.

The Mayor said, "I can see now that Mog is a gentle cat. He can live in the Town Hall with you, Mrs Jones. Here is a badge for him to wear."

The badge was on a silver chain to go round his neck. It said MOG SAVED OUR TOWN.

So Mrs Jones and Mog lived happily ever after in the Town Hall. If you should go to the little town of Carnmog you may see the policeman holding up the traffic while Mog walks through the streets on his way to catch fish in the lake for breakfast. His tail waves above the houses and his whiskers rattle against the upstairs windows. But people know he will not hurt them, because he is a gentle cat.

He loves to play in the lake and sometimes he gets so wet that he sneezes. But Mrs Jones is not going to give him any more yeast.

He is quite big enough already!

The Beautiful Doll's Pram

Geraldine Kaye

One sunny day in the Easter holidays Charlene and Mum and baby Kelso went to the park to meet Aunt Lileeth. Charlene pushed the buggy. Kelso had a new blue Babygro and a fancy bib.

"Gug," he said.

"I wish we had a proper lying-down baby," Charlene said as they crossed on the crossing. "A proper small baby."

The park had grass and grey paths and shady trees. It had swings one way and a rose garden and a café the other.

"Can I go on the swings?" Charlene said. But Aunt Lileeth was already sitting at one of the tables outside the café.

Aunt Lileeth said, "Can this giant really be baby Kelso?" and "My-my, you're a real grown-up girl, Charlene, pushing the buggy and all." Charlene didn't say anything.

Mum got tea and an orange drink on a tray and took out a rusk for Kelso. Then Aunt Lileeth and Mum started talking. Charlene drank her orange and tried to listen. But it was all grown-up stuff and she soon got tired of it.

"Gug," said Kelso. There was rusk on his fancy bib.

"Can I take him to the rose garden over there?" Charlene said.

"All right, but stay where I can see you. Take care now," Mum said, and she went on talking to Aunt Lileeth.

"I wish you could talk, Kelso," Charlene said as she pushed the buggy along the path.

The rose garden had a hedge all round. Inside the hedge were lots of square rose beds with red and yellow and white roses and paths between. Charlene sniffed at the roses and held one down so Kelso could sniff.

"Gug," said Kelso and went to sleep.

Charlene looked over the hedge. One way she could see Mum and Aunt Lileeth and she waved and they waved back and went on talking and talking. The other way she could see a lawn and a shady tree with some big girls sitting under it and talking and talking.

Charlene sat down on a seat. A girl her own age was coming down the path pushing a plum-red pram with a smart white hood and white wheels. It was so big that Charlene didn't even see it was a doll's pram until the girl sat down beside her. Inside was a baby doll, a proper lying-down baby doll.

"I like your pram," Charlene said, turning the buggy away so the girl couldn't see the rusk on Kelso's bib.

"I had it for my birthday. I'm called Elizabeth after the Queen, by the way. I'll show you my doll if you like?"

"Oh yes, please . . ." Charlene said.

Elizabeth lifted the doll from the pram. "Mama," it said. It was the prettiest baby doll Charlene had ever seen, with long dark eyelashes and a lacy pink dress.

"She wets her nappies too," Elizabeth said. "I'll show you in a minute but can I have a turn with your baby first?"

"What sort of turn?" Charlene said.

"Just a little walk," Elizabeth said. "Round the rose garden. You can go one way with my pram and I'll go the other way with your baby in the buggy. What's his name?"

"Kelso," said Charlene. "After a place in Scotland by the way."

Charlene kept her eyes on the

plum-red pram all the time as she
pushed it along the hedge. It was
like a dream, she thought. She
pretended it was *her* doll and *her*
pram and she walked very slowly
to make it last a long time like she
did with sweets. She walked along
one side of the hedge and round
the corner and along the next side

and round the next corner.

She was halfway now, so where was Elizabeth and the buggy and Kelso?

Charlene began to walk faster. Along the hedge and round the corner but she still couldn't see them. She began to run. She ran as fast as she could and the baby doll bounced from side to side and mud got on the white wheels of the pram and then she was back at the seat. The big girls were still talking under the shady tree but there was no sign of Elizabeth or the buggy or Kelso.

"Kelso?" Charlene whispered. Perhaps Elizabeth had meant they should walk round the rose garden twice. She ran off round the rose garden the other way keeping the pram close to the hedge. But when she got back to the seat Kelso still wasn't there.

A big girl was coming across the lawn. "Who said you could play with my sister's doll's pram?" she said, taking hold of it. "Where's Lizzie gone? Don't say she's run off again?"

"Where's Kelso?" Charlene cried all fluttery inside.

"Lizzie . . ." the big girl shouted. "Lizzie, come back here this minute or I'll tell. Lizzie, just wait till I catch you . . ."

Charlene ran off round the rose garden again. Round the first corner and round the next corner. And there was Mum and Aunt Lileeth and the buggy and Kelso still fast asleep.

"Where did you get to, Charlene?" Mum said; she was rather cross. "How come I look up and see this other girl pushing Kelso's buggy?"

"You can see Charlene's sorry," said Aunt Lileeth.

"Gug," said Kelso waking up.

Charlene took off the fancy bib and dried her eyes on the clean side. Faraway, across the rose garden hedge, she could see Elizabeth and

131

the beautiful doll's pram and her big sister still scolding.

They said goodbye to Aunt Lileeth and Charlene pushed the buggy home the same way, following the grey path to the gate and back across the crossing. But it didn't seem the *same* to Charlene. The sky was suddenly so blue above her head and the grass was so green and the pavement was soft as swan's-down under her feet and Kelso was honey-sweet. And she would never let anybody push the buggy again because she was Kelso's sister. And Kelso was her own little brother.

The Happy Lion

Louise Fatio

There was once a very happy lion. His home was not the hot and dangerous plains of Africa where hunters lie in wait with their guns; it was a lovely French town with brown tile roofs and grey gutters. The happy lion had a house in the town zoo, all for himself, with a large rock garden surrounded by a moat, in the middle of the park with flower beds and a bandstand.

Early every morning, François, the keeper's son, stopped on his way to school to say, "*Bonjour*, Happy Lion."

In the afternoons, Monsieur Dupont, the schoolmaster, stopped on his way home to say, "*Bonjour*, Happy Lion."

In the evenings, Madame Pinson, who knitted all day on the bench by the bandstand, never left without saying, "*Au revoir*, Happy Lion."

On summer Sundays, the town band filed into the bandstand to play waltzes and polkas. And the happy lion closed his eyes to listen. He loved music. Everyone

was his friend and came to say
"*Bonjour*" and offer meat and
other titbits.

He *was* a happy lion.

One morning, the happy lion
found that his keeper had
forgotten to close the door of his
house.

"Hmm," he said, "I don't like
that. Anyone may walk in."

"Oh well," he added on second
thought, "maybe I will walk out
myself and see my friends in town.
It will be nice to return their
visits."

So the happy lion walked out
into the park and said, "*Bonjour*,
my friends" to the busy sparrows.

"*Bonjour*, Happy Lion," answered the busy sparrows.

And he said, "*Bonjour*, my friend" to the quick red squirrel who sat on his tail and bit into a walnut.

"*Bonjour*, Happy Lion," said the red squirrel, hardly looking up.

Then the happy lion went into the cobblestone street where he met Monsieur Dupont just around the corner.

"*Bonjour*," he said, nodding in his polite lion way.

"Hoooooooooohhh . . ." answered Monsieur Dupont, and fainted on to the pavement.

"What a silly way to say

bonjour," said the happy lion, and he padded along on his big soft paws.

"*Bonjour*, Mesdames," the happy lion said farther down the street when he saw three ladies he had known at the zoo.

"Huuuuuuuuuuuuuhhhhhh . . ." cried the three ladies, and ran away as if an ogre were after them.

"I can't think," said the happy lion, "what makes them do that. They are always so polite at the zoo."

"*Bonjour*, Madame." The happy lion nodded again when he caught up with Madame Pinson near the greengrocer's.

"Oo la la . . .!" cried Madame Pinson, and threw her shopping bag full of vegetables into the lion's face.

"A-a-a-a-choooooo," sneezed the lion. "People in this town are foolish, as I begin to see."

Now the lion began to hear the joyous sounds of a military march. He turned around the next corner, and there was the town band, marching down the street between two lines of people. Ratatum ratata ratatatum ratatata boom boom.

Before the lion could even nod and say, "*Bonjour*", the music became screams and yells. What a hubbub! Musicians and spectators tumbled into one another in the flight toward doorways and pavement cafés. Soon the street was empty and silent.

The lion sat down and meditated.

"I suppose," he said, "this must be the way people behave when they are not at the zoo."

Then he got up and went on with his stroll in search of a friend who would not faint, or scream, or run away. But the only people he saw were pointing at him excitedly from the highest windows and balconies.

Now what was this new noise the lion heard?

"Toootooooot . . .
hoootoooooootoooooot . . ." went
that noise.

"Hooooot toooooo TOOOOOOO
OOOOOOOOHHHOOO OT . . ."
and it grew more and more noisy.

"It may be the wind," said the
lion. "Unless it is the monkeys
from the zoo, all of them taking a
stroll."

All of a sudden a big red fire
engine burst out of a side street,
and came to a stop, not too far
from the lion. Then a big van came
backing up on the other side of
him with its back door wide open.

The lion just sat down very
quietly, for he did not want to miss

what was going to happen.

The firemen got off the fire engine and advanced very very slowly towards the lion, pulling their big fire hose along. Very slowly they came closer . . . and closer . . . and the fire hose crawled on like a long snake, longer and longer . . .

SUDDENLY, behind the lion, a little voice cried, "*Bonjour*, Happy Lion." It was François, the keeper's son, on his way home from school! He had seen the lion and had come running to him. The happy lion was so VERY HAPPY to meet a friend who did not run and who said "*Bonjour*" that he forgot all about the firemen.

And he never found out what they were going to do, because François put his hand on the lion's great mane and said, "Let's walk back to the park together."

"Yes, let's," purred the happy lion.

So François and the happy lion walked back to the zoo. The firemen followed behind in the fire engine, and the people on the balconies and in the high windows shouted at last, "*BONJOUR*! HAPPY LION!"

From then on the happy lion got the best titbits the town saved for him. But if you opened his door he would not wish to go out visiting again. He was happier to sit in his rock garden while on the other side of the moat Monsieur Dupont, Madame Pinson, and all his old friends came again like polite and sensible people to say "*Bonjour*, Happy Lion." But he was happiest when he saw François walk through the park every afternoon on his way home from school. Then he swished his tail for joy, for François remained always his dearest friend.

Little Old Mrs Pepperpot

Alf Prøysen

There was once an old woman who went to bed at night as old women usually do, and in the morning she woke up as old women usually do. But on this particular morning she found herself shrunk to the size of a pepperpot, and old women don't usually do that. The odd thing was, her name really was Mrs Pepperpot.

"Well, as I'm now the size of a pepperpot, I shall have to make the best of it," she said to herself, for she had no one else to talk to; her husband was out in the fields and all her children were grown up and gone away.

Now she happened to have a great deal to do that day. First of all she had to clean the house, then there was all the washing which was lying in soak and waiting to be done, and lastly she had to make pancakes for supper.

"I must get out of bed somehow," she thought, and, taking hold of a corner of the eiderdown, she started rolling herself up in it. She rolled and rolled until the eiderdown was like a huge sausage, which fell softly on the floor. Mrs Pepperpot crawled out and she hadn't hurt herself a bit.

The first job was to clean the house, but that was quite easy; she just sat down in front of a mousehole and squeaked till the mouse came out.

"Clean the house from top to bottom," she said, "or I'll tell the cat about you." So the mouse cleaned the house from top to bottom.

Mrs Pepperpot called the cat, "Puss! Puss! Puss! Lick out all the plates and dishes or I'll tell the

dog about you." And the cat licked
all the plates and dishes clean.

Then the old woman called the
dog. "Listen, dog; you make the
bed and open the window and I'll
give you a bone as a reward." So
the dog did as he was told, and
when he had finished he sat down
on the front doorstep and waved

his tail so hard he made the step shine like a mirror.

"You'll have to get the bone yourself," said Mrs Pepperpot, "I haven't time to wait on people." She pointed to the windowsill where a large bone lay.

After this she wanted to start her washing. She had put it to soak in the brook, but the brook was almost dry. So she sat down and started muttering in a discontented sort of way:

"I have lived a long time, but in all my born days I never saw the brook so dry. If we don't have a shower soon, I expect everyone will die of thirst." Over and over

again she said it, all the time
looking up at the sky.

At last the raincloud in the sky
got so angry that it decided to
drown the old woman altogether.
But she crawled under a monk's-
hood flower, where she stayed snug
and warm while the rain poured
down and rinsed her clothes clean
in the brook.

Now the old woman started
muttering again, "I have lived a
long time, but in all my born days
I have never known such a feeble
South Wind as we have had lately.
I'm sure if the South Wind started
blowing this minute it couldn't lift
me off the ground, even though I

am no bigger than a pepperpot."

The South Wind heard this and instantly came tearing along, but Mrs Pepperpot hid in an empty badger sett, and from there she watched the South Wind blow all the clothes right up on to her clothesline.

Again she started muttering, "I have lived a long time, but in all my born days I have never seen the sun give so little heat in the middle of the summer. It seems to have lost all its power, that's a fact."

When the sun heard this it turned scarlet with rage and sent down fiery rays to give the old

151

woman sunstroke. But by this time she was safely back in her house, and was sailing about the sink in a saucer. Meanwhile, the furious sun dried all the clothes on the line.

"Now for cooking the supper," said Mrs Pepperpot; "my husband will be back in an hour and, by hook or by crook, thirty pancakes must be ready on the table."

She had mixed the dough for the pancakes in a bowl the day before. Now she sat down beside the bowl and said, "I have always been fond of you, bowl, and I've told all the neighbours that there's not a bowl like you anywhere. I am sure, if you really wanted to, you could walk straight over to the cooking-stove and turn it on."

And the bowl went straight over to the stove and turned it on.

Then Mrs Pepperpot said, "I'll never forget the day I bought my frying pan. There were lots of pans in the shop, but I said, 'If I can't have that pan hanging right over the shop assistant's head, I won't buy any pan at all. For that is the best pan in the whole world, and I'm sure if I were ever in trouble that pan could jump on to the stove by itself.'"

And there and then the frying pan jumped on to the stove. And when it was hot enough, the bowl tilted itself to let the dough run on to the pan.

Then the old woman said, "I once read a fairy-tale about a pancake which could roll along the road. It was the stupidest story that I ever read. But I'm sure the pancake on the pan could easily turn a somersault in the air if it really wanted to."

At this the pancake took a great leap from sheer pride and turned a somersault as Mrs Pepperpot had said. Not only one pancake, but *all* the pancakes did this, and the bowl went on tilting and the pan went on frying until, before the hour was up, there were thirty pancakes on the dish.

Then Mr Pepperpot came home. And, just as he opened the door, Mrs Pepperpot turned back to her usual size. So they sat down and ate their supper.

And the old woman said nothing about having been as small as a pepperpot, because old women don't usually talk about such things.

Mary Kate Climbs a Mountain

Martin Waddell

Mary Kate is Gran's doll – and what an amazing doll she is . . .

"I thought Mary Kate playing with me was just one of your stories!" Pete told Gran. "But it isn't! Mary Kate says she wants to play games."

"Good!" Gran said, looking up from her paper. If she was

surprised, she didn't show it. Pete was the one who was surprised, and Pete wasn't just surprised . . . he was amazed!

"What games will we play?" Pete asked.

"Better ask Mary Kate," Gran said, and she disappeared back inside her paper.

"I don't believe this!" Pete told Mary Kate. "I thought you were one of Gran's pretend stories!"

"I'm not anyone's story," Mary Kate said, sounding a little insulted. "I'm me!"

Mary Kate walked round Pete, and took a good look. It was a long walk for someone Mary Kate's size and there was a lot of Pete to look at. Pete was quite small as little boys go, but compared to Mary Kate Pete was ginormous, almost mega-ginormous in fact.

"You are very big, Pete," Mary Kate said, sounding worried.

"Mum thinks I'm small-ish," said Pete.

"That's how all mums think," Mary Kate said. "It comes of being Mum-size. I'm not Mum-size. I'm Mary-Kate-size, and Mary-Kate-size is quite small . . . so that makes you very big. But not too big yet, I suppose."

"Too big for what?" Pete asked.

"Too big to play with," Mary

Kate said. "Like your gran. I used to play with your gran, but I don't play with her any more. She's too big now to play games with me."

"Gran told me that," Pete said. "But I thought she was making it up."

"We'll play by ourselves, and we won't disturb her," Mary Kate said.

"What game will we play first?" Pete asked Mary Kate.

Mary Kate thought for a bit, and she turned and looked all around Gran's sitting room. Pete watched her hopefully. He'd looked all around the room himself, and he hadn't found anything. Pete hoped that Mary Kate would, otherwise it would be just watching TV and playing with Gran's jigsaw puzzles. There had to be something better than that.

"Let's climb Armchair Mountain!" Mary Kate said.

They were both down on the floor beside Armchair Mountain.

Looking up at the mountain, Pete felt he was smaller than small, almost as small as Mary Kate was . . . at least a part of Pete believed he was Mary-Kate-small, looking up at a mountain. Another part of Pete knew quite well that he wasn't, and went back to being big Pete again . . . big by Mary

Kate standards that is. It was all a bit confusing so Pete didn't bother too much about it. He was much more interested in climbing the mountain Mary Kate had pointed out to him than wondering about being too big to do it.

"We need ropes to climb," Mary Kate said. "It's a huge mountain, and very dangerous, and there isn't a lot to cling on to."

Pete looked around the room.

"Mary Kate wants to climb Armchair Mountain!" he told Gran.

"What mountain?" asked Gran, looking up. "I didn't know there were any mountains in here!"

161

"Armchair Mountain is Grandpa's armchair," Pete explained. "If you are Mary Kate's size, it's a very big mountain."

"Good idea!" said Gran.

"Mary Kate says it is dangerous, because there isn't a lot to cling on to," Pete said. "We might need a rope to climb it, but we haven't got one."

"Use my wool," Gran said, and she gave Pete a ball of wool from her basket.

"We might need other things," Pete told Gran.

So Pete and Gran made a list of things they might need for climbing a mountain, and Pete helped Gran to collect all the things.

CLIMBING KIT FOR PETE AND MARY KATE'S ARMCHAIR MOUNTAIN EXPEDITION

- one handkerchief tent (two persons)
- two emergency ration packs
- one flag to stick on top of the mountain.

"I've got all the things that we need now," Pete told Mary Kate.

"Tell your gran 'thank you' from me," Mary Kate said, and Pete did.

"No bother!" Gran said. "I hope

you and Mary Kate have great fun,
but look out for Big Mountain
Bears, just in case."

"Are there Big Bears on
Armchair Mountain?" Pete asked.
"Real bears, not like my bears at
home?" Pete's bears were Bunkum,
and Retep (Retep is "Peter"
spelled backwards). They were tea-
party-on-the-sofa-living-bears from
a shop. Pete thought real Big
Mountain Bears might be rougher
and tougher.

"You never know with Big
Mountain Bears," Gran said.
"There might be."

"Really Big Bears?" Pete asked
feeling worried about it. He wasn't

sure if he wanted to tackle a Big
Mountain Bear.

"Could be," said Gran. "How
should I know? I've never been up
that mountain. But I'm sure you
can chase off the bears, if they're
there. All you have to do is shout
out BEARBOO and the Big Bears
run away."

Pete asked Mary Kate if she
thought that they could
BEARBOO the Big Bears, and
Mary Kate said she thought that
they could. Mary Kate wasn't
scared of Big Bears, and so Pete
wasn't either.

Pete divided their climbing kit
up so that it was fair. Mary Kate

carried the flag stuck in the back
of her trousers and Pete carried
the rest, because Pete was biggest
and could carry more than Mary
Kate, and anyway Pete was the one
with the pocket that the kit went
into.

"One end round me, and one end
round you!" Mary Kate told Pete,
handing him the rope. Pete could
tie his own knots because Mum
had taught him how to, so Pete
tied the knots for both of them.
Mary Kate wasn't much good at
knots, but Pete hadn't time to
teach her just then.

Mary Kate started to climb up
Armchair Mountain, and Pete

climbed below, holding on to the
end of the rope.

"This is the highest mountain in
all of the land!" Mary Kate
shouted down to Pete.

"What about Everest?" said Pete.
"Dad says that's the highest
mountain there is."

"Everest isn't in this land," Mary
Kate said. "This is Sitting Room
Land, where I live, so I ought to
know."

They climbed up and up, till they
reached Arm Rest Ridge.

"Let's camp here for the night,
Mary Kate!" Pete suggested.
That's what they did. They used
Pete's handkerchief-tent. Pete

fixed one corner of the handkerchief-tent to the button on the back of the chair, and spread the other three corners out. They could just about both go inside.

"It's time we ate some of our rations!" Mary Kate said.

"They are for emergencies," Pete told her.

"I'm hungry," Mary Kate said. "That is an emergency!"

So Mary Kate ate one of the sweeties Gran had given Pete for emergency rations. Pete ate one as well, and they put the other two back in the ration pack in Pete's pocket.

They slept for hours in their

tent. The only noise was the howling of wolves on the sides of the mountains, but there weren't bears about, big or small, so Gran was wrong. Pete knew there weren't Big Bears because both he and Mary Kate kept a lookout for bear tracks. Mary Kate thought the Big Bears might have left Sitting Room Land and gone to live in Gran's bathroom, because Big Bears like eating toothpaste. That's why the toothpaste tubes in Gran's flat were all bendy. Mary Kate told him the Big Mountain Bears squeezed Gran's toothpaste with their big paws but Pete didn't know if it was true.

"Today we climb right to the top!" Pete told Mary Kate the next morning. "It must be today, or we'll run out of rations."

They climbed on and on and then . . .

"Made it!" said Pete.

They stood on the top of the mountain, looking down at Carpet Valley below.

"More food now!" Mary Kate said, when they'd planted the flag.

So they ate up the rest of the rations, and Pete put the wrapping papers back in his pocket, so they wouldn't mess up Gran's clean floor.

"I like it here," Mary Kate said,

but that was because Mary Kate wasn't keeping a lookout, and she hadn't noticed the danger. Pete was in charge of lookout, and he saw the danger at once.

"The sky has gone black so that means there's a storm coming!" Pete told Mary Kate. "We can't pitch our tent here because it will blow off the mountain, and we would be frozen to death if it snows. And we can't climb back down because there isn't time."

"We'll have to jump off the top of the mountains to the valley below!" Mary Kate told Pete.

"It looks a big drop!" Pete said.

It was Mary Kate who thought of

making the parachute, and she told Pete all about it.

Pete made Mary Kate a parachute out of the handkerchief-tent. He tied a different bit of wool on to each corner of the handkerchief, and then he tied them all on to Mary Kate's waist, so in the end Mary Kate looked like a small bundle of wool.

"Be careful you don't hurt yourself," Pete told Mary Kate.

"I'm made of soft stuff!" said Mary Kate. "I don't break."

Mary Kate jumped. She landed down in Carpet Valley, with a bit of a bump, but it was all right.

It was such a soft bump that Gran didn't notice.

Pete stood up to jump off the top of the mountain, down miles and miles and miles to the valley.

"Look out down below!" Pete shouted, and that made Gran look up from her paper at last. She saw Pete standing on the arm of Grandpa's armchair.

"Be careful, Pete," said Gran, getting up from her chair. "You could fall."

Gran lifted Pete down from the chair.

"We climbed Armchair Mountain," Pete explained. "There weren't any Big Bears but there

173

was a storm coming and snow and we'd run out of rations and Mary Kate had to parachute off down to Carpet Valley."

He showed Gran Mary Kate and the handkerchief-tent-parachute, tied on with wool.

"You've made quite a mess of it!" Gran said, running her hands through the wool. There were lots of knots in it, and tangles, left over from being a tent and a parachute and a climbing rope.

"You said we could use it for ropes when we were climbing the mountain," Pete said.

"I didn't know it was going to be part of a parachute too," Gran said. "And you can tell Mary Kate that!"

"It wasn't my idea," Pete said. "It was Mary Kate's."

"Well, perhaps you and Mary Kate can roll the wool back into a ball for my knitting," Gran said.

Pete whispered what Gran had said to Mary Kate.

"Mary Kate says she can't do things when you are looking!" Pete told Gran.

"I didn't hear her say that!" Gran said. "She was never so fussy before!"

"Well, she did," said Pete. "You're grown-up, so she can't do things like putting wool back into ball-shape while you are sitting there watching."

"That's too bad," Gran said. "I suppose we'll just have to do it ourselves."

In the end Gran and Pete re-rolled all the wool and put Mary Kate back on the chair for a sleep, because she felt tired. Gran read Pete his story and then they went for a walk and Gran got some sausages and then Mum came to take Pete home.

"Don't wake Mary Kate!" Pete said, when Mum went to sit down.

"I wouldn't dream of disturbing Mary Kate!" Mum said, sitting on the arm of the chair.

"Then don't talk so loud," Pete said. "If you wake her up, you'll have to tell her a story before she goes back to sleep."

Then Pete went to look for one of the books he kept at Gran's. He thought he could listen too when Mum read it to Mary Kate, and put in any bits Mum skipped out. Mum sometimes skipped bits when she was in a hurry, but he always knew what they were and made her put them back in. Pete liked all the words to be there in his stories.

"You'll get your story at home, Pete," Mum said.

"I think Mary Kate might be

awake," Pete said.

"If she wakes up, Gran will tell her a story," Mum said. "We absolutely haven't time for a doll's storytime. The dinner is on, and it will burn! So tough luck, Mary Kate!"

"You seem to like Mary Kate," Mum said, in the car.

"Yes, I do," Pete said. "We played a good game." And Pete told Mum how they'd climbed Armchair Mountain together.

"There are Big Bears in Gran's flat but it's all right because Mary Kate is very brave, just like me. We know how to scare off Big

Mountain Bears," Pete said, sounding just-a-bit anxious.

"I don't believe that there are Big Mountain Bears in Gran's flat," Mum said. "Gran makes up things like that, but you don't have to believe her. I don't want you being scared of Big Bears."

"I'm not scared of Big Bears," Pete told her. "I know how to look after Big Bears. You shout BEARBOO and they go and eat toothpaste instead." Pete told Mum all about the toothpaste that was squeezed in Gran's bathroom, which proved there were bears in Gran's flat.

"All right, I give up on the

bears!" Mum said. "But make sure you and Mary Kate and Gran's indoor bears don't have such big adventures that you wreck poor Gran's flat and not just her wool and her toothpaste."

"We never touched Gran's toothpaste, Mum," Pete said. "It was the Big Bears."

"Gran said you were jumping off Granpa's armchair," Mum said. "I suppose you blame that on the Big Bears as well?"

"That was Mary Kate," Pete said.

"I hope she didn't hurt herself," Mum said. "Jumping off mountains sounds dangerous to me. I know you wouldn't do it."

"Mary Kate didn't hurt herself because she is made of soft stuff," Pete told Mum. "That's what Mary Kate says."

"I see!" said Mum. "That's very sensible of Mary Kate."

"Mary Kate is very sensible," Pete said. Then he thought for a bit, and he said, "We're doing something very sensible tomorrow, but I'm not going to tell you what it is, because it is our secret."

Then he thought a bit more.

"Mary Kate thinks we might need my bricks!" Pete said. "But not the Bad Brick!"

"Why not?" Mum asked.

"The Bad Brick might be scared of Big Mountain Bears," he told Mum.

"That's just like the Bad Brick!" Mum said.

So on Tuesday morning Pete took his bricks with him to Gran's but he made a Pete-mistake. He took the Bad Brick!

Milly-Molly-Mandy Camps Out

Joyce Lankester Brisley

Once upon a time Milly-Molly-Mandy and Toby the dog went down to the village, to Miss Muggins's shop, on an errand for Mother; and as they passed Mr Blunt's corn-shop Milly-Molly-Mandy saw something new in the little garden at the side. It looked like a small, shabby sort of tent, with a slit in the top and a big checked patch sewn on the side.

Milly-Molly-Mandy wondered what it was doing there. But she didn't see Billy Blunt anywhere about, so she couldn't ask him.

When she came out of Miss Muggins's shop she had another good look over the palings into the Blunt's garden. And while she was looking Billy Blunt came out of their house door with some old rugs and a pillow in his arms.

"Hullo, Billy!" said Milly-Molly-Mandy. "What's that tent-thing?"

"It's a tent," said Billy Blunt, not liking its being called "thing".

"But what's it for?" asked Milly-

Molly-Mandy.

"It's mine," said Billy Blunt.

"Yours? Your very own? Is it?" said Milly-Molly-Mandy. "Ooh, do let me come and look at it!"

"You can if you want to," said Billy Blunt. "I'm going to sleep in it tonight – camp out."

Milly-Molly-Mandy was very interested indeed. She looked at it well, outside and in. She could only just stand up in it. Billy Blunt had spread an old mackintosh for a groundsheet, and there was a box in one corner to hold a bottle of water and a mug, and his electric torch, and such necessary things; and when the front flap of the tent was closed you couldn't see anything outside, except a tiny bit of sky and some green leaves through the tear in the top.

Milly-Molly-Mandy didn't want to come out a bit, but Billy Blunt wanted to put his bedding in.

"Isn't it beautiful! Where did you get it, Billy?" she asked.

"My cousin gave it to me," said Billy Blunt. "Used it when he went on cycling holidays. He's got a new one now. I put that patch on myself."

Milly-Molly-Mandy thought she could have done it better; but still it was quite good for a boy, so she duly admired it, and offered to mend the other place. But Billy Blunt didn't think it was worth it, as it would only tear away again – and he liked a bit of air, anyhow.

"Shan't you feel funny out here all by yourself when everybody else is asleep?" said Milly-Molly-

Mandy. "Oh, I wish I had a tent too!" Then she said goodbye and ran with Toby the dog back home to the nice white cottage with the thatched roof, thinking of the tent all the way.

She didn't see little-friend-Susan as she passed the Moggs's cottage along the road; but when she got as far as the meadow she saw her swinging her baby sister on the big gate.

"Hullo, Milly-Molly-Mandy! I was just looking for you," said little-friend-Susan, lifting Baby Moggs down. And Milly-Molly-Mandy told her all about Billy Blunt's new tent, and how he was going to sleep out, and how she wished she had a tent too.

Little-friend-Susan was almost as interested as Milly-Molly-Mandy. "Can't we make a tent and play in it in your meadow?" she said. "It would be awful fun!"

So they got some bean-poles and bits of sacking from the barn and dragged them down into the meadow. And they had great fun that day trying to make a tent; only they couldn't get it to stay up properly.

Next morning little-friend-Susan came to play "tents" in the meadow again. And this time they tried with an old counterpane,

which Mother had given them, and
two kitchen chairs; and they
managed to rig up quite a good
tent by laying the poles across the
chair-backs and draping the
counterpane over. They fastened
down the spread-out sides with
stones; and the ends, where the
chairs were, they hung with sacks.
And there they had a perfectly
good tent, really quite big enough
for two – so long as the two were
small, and didn't mind being a bit
crowded!

They were just sitting in it,
eating apples and pretending they
had no other home to live in, when
they heard a *"Hi!"*-ing from the

gate; and when they peeped out there was Billy Blunt, with a great bundle in his arms, trying to get the gate open. So they ran across the grass and opened it for him.

"What have you got? Is it your tent? Did you sleep out last night?" asked Milly-Molly-Mandy.

"Look here," said Billy Blunt, "do you think your father would mind, supposing I pitched my tent in your field? My folk don't like it in our garden – say it looks too untidy."

Milly-Molly-Mandy was quite sure Father would not mind. So Billy Blunt put the bundle down inside the gate and went off to ask

(for of course you never camp
anywhere without saying "please"
to the owner first). And Father
didn't mind a bit, so long as no
papers or other rubbish were left
about.

So Billy Blunt set up his tent
near the others', which was not
too far from the nice white cottage
with the thatched roof (because
it's funny what a long way off from
everybody you feel when you've
got only a tent round you at
night!). And then he went to fetch
his other goods; and Milly-Molly-
Mandy and little-friend-Susan sat
in his tent, and wished and wished
that their mothers would let them

sleep out in the meadow that night.

When Billy Blunt came back with his rugs and things (loaded up on his box on wheels) they asked him if it were very creepy-feeling to sleep out of doors.

And Billy Blunt (having slept out once) said, "Oh, you soon get used to it," and asked why they didn't try it in their tent.

So then Milly-Molly-Mandy and little-friend-Susan looked at each other, and said firmly, "Let's ask!" So little-friend-Susan went with Milly-Molly-Mandy up to the nice white cottage with the thatched roof, where Mother was just putting a treacle tart into the oven.

She looked very doubtful when Milly-Molly-Mandy told her what they wanted to do. Then she shut the oven door, and wiped her hands, and said, well, she would just come and look at the tent they had made first. And when she had looked and considered, she said, well, if it were still very fine and dry by the evening perhaps Milly-Molly-Mandy might sleep out there, just for once. And Mother found a rubber groundsheet and some old blankets and cushions, and gave them to her.

Then Milly-Molly-Mandy went

with little-friend-Susan to the
Moggs's cottage, where Mrs Moggs
was just putting their potatoes on
to boil.

She looked very doubtful at first;
and then she said, well, if Milly-
Molly-Mandy's mother had been
out to see, and thought it was all
right, and if it were a *very* nice,
fine evening, perhaps little-friend-
Susan might sleep out, just for
once.

So all the rest of that day the
three were very busy, making
preparations and watching the sky.
And when they all went home for
supper the evening was beautifully
still and warm, and without a

single cloud.

So, after supper, they all met together again in the meadow, in the sunset. And they shut and tied up the meadow-gate. (It was all terribly exciting!)

And Mother came out, with Father and Grandpa and Grandma and Uncle and Aunty, to see that all was right, and their groundsheets well spread under their bedding.

Then Milly-Molly-Mandy and little-friend-Susan crawled into their tent, and Billy Blunt crawled into his tent. And presently Milly-Molly-Mandy crawled out again in her pyjamas, and ran about with bare feet on the grass with Toby the dog; and then little-friend-Susan and Billy Blunt, in their pyjamas, crawled out and ran about too (because it feels so very nice, and so sort of new, to be running about under the sky in your pyjamas!).

And Father and Mother and Grandpa and Grandma and Uncle and Aunty laughed, and looked on as if they wouldn't mind doing it too, if they weren't so grown-up.

Then Mother said, "Now I think it's time you campers popped into bed. Good night!" And they went off home.

So Milly-Molly-Mandy and little-friend-Susan called "Good night!" and crawled into one tent, and Billy Blunt caught Toby the dog and crawled into the other.

And the trees outside grew slowly blacker and blacker until they couldn't be seen at all; and the owls hooted; and a far-away cow moo-ed; and now and then Toby the dog wuffed, because he thought he heard a rabbit; and sometimes Milly-Molly-Mandy or little-friend-Susan squeaked, because they thought they felt a spider walking on them. And once Billy Blunt called out to ask if they were still awake, and they said they were, and was he? and he said of course he was.

And then at last they all fell asleep.

And in no time at all the sun was shining through their tents, telling them to wake up and come out, because it was the next day.

And Billy Blunt and Milly-Molly-Mandy and little-friend-Susan DID enjoy that camping-out night!

Wil's Tail

Hazel Hutchins

Wilmot James Edward Hutchins was the sixth wolf from the left at the school Christmas Concert. When the concert was over everyone said what a good Christmas forest creature he'd been and everyone admired his costume. Wil admired his costume too – especially the tail.

It was a wonderful tail. His

mother had made it from the belt
of her old fake-fur coat. Wil
himself had sewed it to the seat of
his favourite corduroy trousers. It
was the kind of tail that hung
"just right" and swung "just
right". It was the kind of a tail
with which Wil could slink or
jump; the kind of tail he could
twirl or drape; the kind of tail he
could curl smoothly around him. It
had patterns and lines and colours
in it that Wil had never even
thought about before, and it was
softer than anything he'd ever
known.

When Wil got home, he hung the
wolf mask on his bedroom wall.

He put the sweater (his dad's) back
in the big dresser drawer. He put
the mittens (his sister's) and the
moccasins (his mother's) back in
the closet where they belonged.
But he kept the tail.

The next day was Christmas Eve.
Wil helped wrap presents and eat
biscuits. When evening came, his

family went to a party at the neighbours. Wil's dad wore his smart jeans. Wil's mum wore her party blouse. Wil's sister wore sixteen hairslides. And Wil wore his tail.

He wore it during supper and he wore it during games and he wore it during carol singing. The neighbours thought it a bit strange, but they were too polite to say anything.

Wil was tired when he got home. He hung up his stocking and rolled into bed. His tail rolled into bed too, all except the tip which hung out over the edge.

On Christmas morning, Wil's

family hugged and kissed and opened presents and ate breakfast. They went to the cousins for the day. Wil's dad wore his Christmas tie. Wil's mum wore her Christmas perfume. Wil's sister wore her Christmas brooch and her Christmas socks. Wil wore his Christmas tail.

Aunt Beth nearly had a heart attack when she stepped on it in the kitchen.

On Boxing Day, the family ate leftovers and played 327 games of draughts. The next day they went shopping in the city. Everyone wore their everyday, ordinary clothes. Wil wore his tail.

The tip of it got caught in the escalator of Krumings' department store. A loud warning bell went off. Two security people and three maintenance personnel worked to free the mechanism and every shopper in the whole store came to see the boy whose tail had been caught between the second and third floors.

For the rest of the week Wil stayed at home with his tail. He repaired it with an extra piece, so it was longer than ever. He built a den in the basement. He took long naps in front of the fire with the cat. And he waited for New Year's Eve.

On New Year's Eve the family always went skating on Whitefish Lake. Wil was planning on wearing his tail. He could just see himself streaking down the lake in the darkness; the wind rushing smoothly against his face and his tail flying far out behind.

But when New Year's Eve came and he tried to tuck his tail up under his sweater, his mother looked at him and shook her head.

"No," she said. "It's dangerous. You'll trip over it and fall and so will everybody else."

Wil appealed to his father.

"No," he said. "It's dangerous. When you go and warm up at the bonfire you're likely to set yourself ablaze."

"But it's part of me!" said Wil.

His parents did not agree.

"All right," said Wil. "I'll wear it but I won't go skating and I won't go near the fire."

His parents gave in.

Whitefish Lake on New Year's Eve was wonderful. People from all over came to skate and laugh and warm themselves around an enormous bonfire. Wil climbed a little hill between the lake and the river which flowed beyond. He listened to the wonderful sound of skate-blades on ice. He watched skaters passing hockey pucks,

turning figures of eight, and
playing tick. Just when he could
stand it no longer and had decided
to take off his tail and put on his
skates, he heard shouting behind
him.

"Someone's fallen through the
river ice!" called the man.

"We can't reach them. A rope. A
long scarf. Help! Anyone, please!"
called the woman.

Wil thought for only a moment.
He reached behind him and pulled
with all his might. With a rip his
tail came loose. He raced down the
slope. The woman took it without
a word and disappeared into the
darkness.

Wil never did get to go skating on Whitefish Lake that New Year's Eve. By the time all the excitement died down, it was time for his family to go home.

But he did get his tail back. The woman who'd taken it made a special point of bringing it back to him. It was sodden and torn and about four feet longer than it had been to start with. Wil didn't care. His tail had actually saved someone's life!

The tail sits, these days, curled up in a special place, right in the middle of Wil's bedroom shelf – a heroic Christmas tail.

Get Lost, Betsey!

Malorie Blackman

Betsey hopped from foot to foot as if her toes were on fire. Today was going to be an excellent day! Betsey and her family were all going to the market – and oh, how Betsey loved the market! But there was an extra special reason why Betsey was so excited.

"Dad's coming home soon!" Betsey beamed.

"Not until next week, Betsey," Sherena reminded her.

"But next week is sooner rather than later," Betsey pointed out.

Dad was abroad studying to be a doctor and it'd been ages since Betsey had last seen him. Although he sent lots of letters and phoned every weekend, it just wasn't the same.

But at last he was coming home.

That's why Betsey's whole family were going to market, to get in all of Dad's favourite foods and to buy other provisions to make him feel really welcome.

"Hurry up, Sherena. You're too slow! If we wait for you, we'll never get to town." Betsey ran over to Sherena and started tugging up the zip at the back of her dress.

"OUCH!" Sherena yelled. "Betsey, you're supposed to zip up the dress, not my skin!"

"I'm only trying to help," said Betsey.

"Then get lost and leave me to do it," said Sherena. "Your kind of help is too painful."

Betsey raced into Desmond's room.

"Desmond! You're not ready. Hurry up!" said Betsey.

"I just need to put my shoes on," said Desmond.

"I'll get them for you," Betsey offered.

Betsey saw Desmond's shoes under his bed and ran past him to get them.

"OW! Betsey, those are my toes, not the carpet," Desmond yelled as Betsey trod on his foot!

"It's OK, you've got five more on that foot!" said Betsey, pointing to the foot she *hadn't* stepped on.

"That's not funny!" fumed Desmond.

"Don't be such a grouch, potato head!" said Betsey.

"I'll stop being a grouch if you go away, get lost, close the door on your way out, put an egg in your

shoe and beat it, make like a tree
and leave!" Desmond said.

"All right! I'll go. But I don't care
what you say to me today, because
we're going to town. *And Dad's
coming home soon!*" Betsey smiled.

Betsey darted out of the room.

SMACK! She crashed straight
into Sherena. And was Sherena
pleased? No, she wasn't.

"Betsey, why don't you watch
where you're going?" snapped
Sherena.

"She's a real pest, isn't she?"
Desmond agreed.

"That's quite enough from both
of you," Gran'ma Liz appeared
from nowhere and glared at

Sherena and Desmond. "You two say sorry to your sister."

"Sorry, Betsey," Sherena and Desmond said at once.

They'd both seen that look on Gran'ma Liz's face before and they weren't about to argue!

"Now let's get going!" smiled Gran'ma Liz.

And at last they were off.

When they got off the bus in town, Betsey hardly knew where to look first. All different kinds of fish and flowers and food and fruits filled the market stalls. Paw-paws, mangoes, bananas, cherries, sugar apples and coconuts on some stalls. Swordfish, flying fish, red mullet and salt fish on others. Sweet potatoes, yams, breadfruits, green bananas, eddoes and okras on still more. Betsey didn't even want to blink in case she missed something.

"Gran'ma Liz! Isn't it extra-amazing?" asked Betsey, her eyes wider than wide.

"Yes, child," smiled Gran'ma Liz. "And tiring! And noisy!"

Betsey and her family weaved their way through the masses of people, looking at stall after stall.

"Betsey, stay close to me. I don't want you wandering off," said Gran'ma Liz.

"No, Gran'ma."

"Mam, I'm just going to do some window shopping," said Sherena.

"I think I'll join you," said Desmond.

"Can I come? Let me come!" said Betsey.

"No way!" Desmond and Sherena said at once.

Gran'ma Liz looked at Sherena and Desmond. "You two aren't being very kind to your sister today. Betsey, go along with them, but don't give them any trouble."

Betsey grinned up at Desmond and Sherena. She was happy about going with them, even if they weren't.

"I'll meet you three at Joe's ice cream stand in an hour," said Mam, glancing down at her watch.

"Come on then, Betsey," tutted Sherena.

And off Desmond and Sherena marched. Betsey had to trot to keep up with them but she didn't mind. It was better than being with the grown-ups!

"Keep up with us, Betsey," said Desmond. "We don't want you slowing us down."

"Don't worry," said Betsey.

On the very next stall there were coconut cakes, all kinds of doughnuts, fresh biscuits and her favourite – banana fritters! They

218

all smelt so scrumptious. Betsey stopped and breathed deeply to get the full effect.

"Look at these!" Betsey called out to her brother and sister who were now some way ahead of her.

"Betsey, get a move on," Sherena called back before she carried on walking.

Betsey ran to catch up with them – and then she saw it! A toy stall! There were rows and rows of rag dolls, bean bags, playing cards, bouncing balls and . . . *marbles*.

Betsey had never seen so many marbles. Hundreds and hundreds of them piled up in buckets. Big ones, little ones, bright ones, glittering ones, marbles that were all one colour and marbles where all the colours fought for space to shine.

"D'you like my marbles?" smiled the woman on the stall.

"Oh yes!" breathed Betsey. "They're beautiful."

"Bring your mam along and I'll sell you some," said the woman.

Mam! Betsey looked around quickly. Where were Sherena and Desmond? Where were Mam and Gran'ma Liz? She couldn't see any of them.

Betsey jumped up and down, trying to see over the heads of all the grown-ups around her, but they were too tall. Betsey's heart suddenly began to hammer in her chest. She raced forward, looking for Desmond and Sherena.

They were nowhere to be found. Betsey ran past stall after stall but . . . nothing. She turned around but she didn't see anything or anyone she recognised.

"Botheration!" said Betsey. "Botheration! Botheration!" She said it two more times!

"I'll go back and try to find Mam and Gran'ma Liz," Betsey decided.

Betsey headed back the way she'd just come but that didn't do any good either. There was noise and bustle and fuss everywhere

Betsey turned. The market wasn't a wonderful place any more. It was big and noisy and frightening. Betsey began to sniff. Her eyes started to sting with tears.

"If you cry, you won't see anything at all," Betsey muttered sternly to herself.

But it didn't help.

All Betsey wanted to do now was find Mam and go home.

"Hello, sugar. Did you find your Mam? Are you going to buy some of my marbles?"

Betsey turned her head. She was in front of the toy stall again. The woman behind the stall smiled at Betsey – and that was it. Betsey

burst into tears.

"What's the matter?"

Immediately the woman came out from behind her stall and squatted down in front of Betsey. "Are you all right?"

"I can't find my mam," Betsey wiped her eyes.

"Hhmm!" said the woman. "I

think the best thing to do is find a policeman. D'you agree?"

Betsey nodded. The stall woman stood up and looked around.

"There's one. OFFICER!"

A policeman came over to the toy stall.

"What's the problem?" asked the policeman, smiling kindly at Betsey.

"I can't find my mam," said Betsey.

"Where d'you live?" asked the policeman.

Betsey had just opened her mouth to tell him, when,

"BETSEY!"

And Betsey was swept off her

feet and hugged so tightly by her mam that she could hardly breathe. Betsey looked around. Sherena, Desmond and Gran'ma Liz were all trying to hug her too!

"Elizabeth Ruby Biggalow! You had us all worried sick," said Gran'ma Liz.

"I know this morning, we told you to get lost . . ." began Sherena.

"But we didn't mean it," finished Desmond.

"Sherena and Desmond, the next time you take your sister somewhere with you, don't wander off and leave her to get lost," said Mam firmly.

"I wasn't lost. I knew exactly

where I was," said Betsey. "I was in the market, looking for all of you. That means you were the ones who were lost, not me!"

"Betsey," Sherena shook her head as everyone else laughed. "I wonder about you sometimes. I really do."

The Little Witch

Margaret Mahy

The big city was dark. Even the streetlights were out. All day people had gone up and down, up and down; cars and buses had roared and rattled busily along. But now they had all gone home to bed, and only the wind, the shadows, and a small kitten wandered in the wide, still streets.

The kitten chased a piece of paper, pretending it was a mouse.

He patted at it with his paws and it flipped behind a rubbish bin. Quick as a wink he leaped after it, and then forgot it because he had found something else.

"What is this?" he asked the wind, "here asleep behind the rubbish bin? I have never seen it before."

The wind was bowling a newspaper along, but he dropped it and came to see. The great stalking shadows looked down from everywhere.

"Ah," said the wind, "it is a witch . . . see her broomstick . . . but she is only a very small one."

The wind was right. It was a very

small witch – a baby one.

The witch heard the wind in her sleep and opened her eyes. Suddenly she was awake.

Far above, the birds peered down at the street below.

"Look!" said the shadows to the sparrows under the eaves. "Look at the little witch; she is such a little witch to be all alone."

"Let me see!" a baby sparrow peeped sleepily.

"Go to sleep!" said his mother. "I didn't hatch you out of the egg to peer at witches all night long."

She snuggled him back into her warm feathers.

But there was no one to snuggle

a little witch, wandering cold in
the big empty streets, dragging a
broom several sizes too big for her.
The kitten sprang at the broom.
Then he noticed something.

"Wind!" he cried. "See –
wherever this witch walks, she
leaves a trail of flowers."

Yes, it is true! The little witch had lots of magic in her, but she had not learned to use it properly, or to hide it, any more than she had learned to talk.

So wherever she put her feet mignonette grew, and rosemary, violets, lily of the valley, and tiny pink-and-white roses . . . all through the streets, and all across the road . . .

Butterflies came, from far and wide, to dance and drink.

"Who is that down there?" asked a young moth.

"It is a baby witch who has made these fine, crimson feast-rooms for us," a tattered old moth answered.

The wind followed along, playing and juggling with the flowers and their sweet smells. "I shall sweep these all over the city," he said. In their sleep, people smelled the flowers and smiled, dreaming happily.

Now the witch looked up at the tall buildings; windows looked down at her with scorn, and their square sharp shapes seemed angry to her. She pointed her finger at them. Out of the cracks and chinks suddenly crept long twining vines and green leaves. Slowly flowers opened on them . . . great crimson flowers like roses, smelling of honey.

The little witch laughed, but in a moment she became solemn. She was so alone. Then the kitten scuttled and pounced at her bare, pink heels, and the little witch knew she had a friend. Dragging her broom for the kitten to chase, she wandered on, leaving a trail of flowers.

Now the little witch stood in the street very small and lost, and cold in her blue smock and bare feet.

She pointed up at the city clock tower, and it became a huge fir tree, while the clock face turned into a white nodding owl and flew away!

The owl flew as fast as the wind to a tall dark castle perched high

233

on a hill. There at a window sat a slim, tired, witch-woman, looking out into the night. "Where, oh where, is my little baby witch?"

"Whoo! Whoo!" cried the owl. "There is a little witch down in the city and she is enchanting everything. What will people say tomorrow?"

The witch-woman rode her broomstick through the sky and over the city, looking eagerly down through the mists. Far below she could see the little witch running and hiding in doorways, while the kitten chased after her.

Down flew the witch-woman – down, down to a shop doorway.

The little witch and the kitten stopped and stared.

"Why," said the witch-woman, in her dark velvety voice, "you are my own dear little witch . . . my lost little witch!" She held out her arms and the little witch ran into them. She wasn't lost any more.

The witch-woman looked around at the enchanted city, and she smiled. "I'll leave it as it is," she said, "for a surprise tomorrow."

Then she gathered the little witch on to her broomstick, and the kitten jumped on too, and off they went to their tall castle home, with windows as deep as night, and lived there happily ever after.

And the next day when the people got up and came out to work, the city was full of flowers and the echoes of laughter.

ACKNOWLEDGEMENTS

The publishers wish to thank the following for permission to reproduce copyright material:

Joan Aiken: for "The Baker's Cat" from *A Necklace of Raindrops* by Joan Aiken, Jonathan Cape. Copyright © Joan Aiken Enterprises Ltd, by permission of A M Heath on behalf of the author.

Laurence Anholt: for *Daft Jack and the Bean Stack* [one of twelve books in the *Seriously Silly* series] Orchard Books (1996), by permission of The Watts Publishing Group.

Hazel Hutchins: for "Wil's Tail", first published in *The Oxford Christmas Story Book*, Oxford University Press (1990), by permission of the author.

Malorie Blackman: for "Get Lost Betsey" from *Magic Betsey* by Malorie Blackman, Picadilly Press, pp. 29–42. Copyright © Malorie Blackman 1994, by permission of A M Heath & Company Ltd on behalf of the author.

Geraldine Kaye: for "The Beautiful Doll's Pram" from *Birthdays in Small Street* by Geraldine Kaye, Methuen Children's Books. Copyright © 1993 Geraldine Kaye, by permission of Egmont Children's Books Ltd.

Penelope Lively: for "The Martian and the Supermarket". Copyright © 1992 Penelope Lively, by permission of Hodder and Stoughton Ltd.

Arnold Lobel: for "Down the Hill" from *Frog and Toad All Year* by Arnold Lobel [first published by World's Work Ltd], Mammoth. Copyright © 1976 Arnold Lobel, by permission of Egmont Children's Books Ltd and HarperCollins, Inc.

Margaret Mahy: for "Mrs Bartelmy's Pet" from *The Second Margaret Mahy Story Book*, J M Dent, 1973, by permission of Orion Publishing Group Ltd; and "The Little Witch" from *A Lion in the Meadows* by Margaret Mahy, J M Dent, by permission of Orion Publishing Group Ltd.

Alf Prøysen: for "Little Old Mrs Pepperpot" from *Little Old Mrs Pepperpot*, Hutchinson, 1959, by permission of Random House Group Ltd.

Catherine Storr: for "Little Polly Riding Hood" from *Clever Polly and the Stupid Wolf* by Catherine Storr, 1979, by permission of Faber and Faber Ltd.

ACKNOWLEDGEMENTS

Martin Waddell: for "Mary Kate Climbs a Mountain" from *The Adventures of Pete and Mary* by Martin Waddell, illustrated by Terry Milne, pp. 19–38. Copyright © 1997 Martin Waddell, by permission of Walker Books Ltd.

Every effort has been made to trace the copyright holders but where this has not been possible or where any error has been made the publishers will be pleased to make the necessary arrangement at the first opportunity.

More top stories for five year olds
can be found in

Magical Stories
for Five Year Olds

Chosen by Helen Paiba

Magical stories include:

The Mermaid Who Lost
Her Crown

Phillipippa's Magic Broom

The Gigantic Badness

Sam Pig Finds a Fortune

The Boy With Two Shadows

More top stories for five year olds
can be found in

Animal Stories
for Five Year Olds
Chosen by Helen Paiba

Exciting stories include:

Elephant Big and Elephant Little

Mr and Mrs Pig's Evening Out

The Dog Who Frightened the Sea

Milly-Molly-Mandy's Hedgehog Baby

Sarah Squirrel's Big Test

More top stories for six year olds
can be found in

Funny Stories
for Six Year Olds

Chosen by Helen Paiba

Hilarious stories include:

The Nasty Case of Dragonitus

Perfect Peter's Horrid Day

The Pig Who Fell in Love

Dilly the Dinosaur's
Television Trouble

The Famous Flying Fishcake
Bird

More top stories for six year olds
can be found in

Magical Stories
for Six Year Olds

Chosen by Helen Paiba

Magical stories include:

The Boy Who Wasn't Bad
Enough

Lindalou and Her Golden Gift

The Sandboat That Sailed Away

Greedy Gregory and the
Tooth Fairy

The Man Whose Mother
Was a Pirate

A selected list of titles available from Macmillan Children's Books

The prices shown below are correct at the time of going to press.
However, Macmillan Publishers reserves the right to show new retail
prices on covers, which may differ from those previously advertised.

Adventure Stories for Five Year Olds	978-0-330-39137-5	£4.99
Animal Stories for Five Year Olds	978-0-330-39125-2	£4.99
Bedtime Stories for Five Year Olds	978-0-330-48366-7	£4.99
Funny Stories for Five Year Olds	978-0-330-39124-5	£4.99
Magical Stories for Five Year Olds	978-0-330-39122-1	£4.99
Adventure Stories for Six Year Olds	978-0-330-39138-2	£4.99
Animal Stories for Six Year Olds	978-0-330-36859-9	£4.99
Bedtime Stories for Six Year Olds	978-0-330-48368-1	£4.99
Funny Stories for Six Year Olds	978-0-330-36857-5	£4.99
Magical Stories for Six Year Olds	978-0-330-36858-2	£4.99
Adventure Stories for Seven Year Olds	978-0-330-39139-9	£4.99
Animal Stories for Seven Year Olds	978-0-330-35494-3	£4.99
Funny Stories for Seven Year Olds	978-0-330-34945-1	£4.99
Scary Stories for Seven Year Olds	978-0-330-34943-7	£4.99
School Stories for Seven Year Olds	978-0-330-48378-0	£4.99
Adventure Stories for Eight Year Olds	978-0-330-39140-5	£4.99
Animal Stories for Eight Year Olds	978-0-330-35495-0	£4.99
Funny Stories for Eight Year Olds	978-0-330-34946-8	£4.99
Scary Stories for Eight Year Olds	978-0-330-34944-4	£4.99
School Stories for Eight Year Olds	978-0-330-48379-7	£4.99
Adventure Stories for Nine Year Olds	978-0-330-39141-2	£4.99
Animal Stories for Nine Year Olds	978-0-330-37493-4	£4.99
Funny Stories for Nine Year Olds	978-0-330-37491-0	£4.99
Scary Stories for Nine Year Olds	978-0-330-37492-7	£4.99
Adventure Stories for Ten Year Olds	978-0-330-39142-9	£4.99
Animal Stories for Ten Year Olds	978-0-330-39128-3	£4.99
Funny Stories for Ten Year Olds	978-0-330-39127-6	£4.99
Scary Stories for Ten Year Olds	978-0-330-39126-9	£4.99

All Pan Macmillan titles can be ordered from our website,
www.panmacmillan.com, or from your local bookshop
and are also available by post from:

Bookpost, PO Box 29, Douglas, Isle of Man IM99 1BQ

Credit cards accepted. For details:
Telephone: 01624 677237
Fax: 01624 670923
Email: bookshop@enterprise.net
www.bookpost.co.uk

Free postage and packing in the United Kingdom